"Relax, sweethear[...]

Trent spoke softly as h[...] in the close confines of the car. "You're twenty-eight, a big girl. Your family won't worry if you're out late."

Filomena sighed. "I don't want them eyeing me at the breakfast table tomorrow. Besides," she said in her usual forthright manner, "*we* hardly know each other, and I'm not about to let you seduce me in the front seat of your car."

"How about the back seat?" He nuzzled her ear. "God, you smell good."

"Trent . . ." But she heard the good-natured resignation in his voice. He wasn't going to push her any harder that night. She was surprised to discover how much that disappointed her. . . .

Jayne Ann Krentz is one of North America's most prolific and popular authors. Though she's written more than fifty books—under her own name as well as the pseudonyms Stephanie James and Jayne Castle—each and every one is special to her. In her latest Temptation Jayne sets out to prove that you can indeed go home again—but sometimes with unexpected results!

Books by Jayne Ann Krentz

Don't miss any of our special offers. Write to us at the following address for information on our newest releases.

Harlequin Reader Service
901 Fuhrmann Blvd., P.O. Box 1397, Buffalo, NY 14240
Canadian address: P.O. Box 603,
Fort Erie, Ont. L2A 5X3

The Main Attraction

JAYNE ANN KRENTZ

Harlequin Books

TORONTO • NEW YORK • LONDON
AMSTERDAM • PARIS • SYDNEY • HAMBURG
STOCKHOLM • ATHENS • TOKYO • MILAN

Published June 1987

ISBN 0-373-25257-9

Printed in Canada

Prologue

TRENT RAVINDER STOOD in the deep shadows of the old lodge building and listened to the whisper of wind in the trees while he watched a redheaded elfin queen take a secret midnight swim.

She was a very charming elf: small, slender, mischievous, intriguing and maddening. He had been trying to get a good grasp on her for days, but she'd always managed to slide through his fingers whenever he'd gotten close.

Elf magic.

She thought she was alone tonight, and she would have been if Trent had not decided to try working off some of his restlessness by taking a midnight walk. But luck or fate or simple coincidence had brought him around the corner of the lodge just in time to see her glide beneath the surface of the pool. Trent had frozen the instant he'd sensed her presence, afraid to disturb the magic.

He stood watching her frolic by herself until she emerged at last from the water. Pale, silvered light gleamed on her soft breasts and the sensual curve of her flanks.

When she reached for a towel, Trent debated whether to make his presence known. It was, after all, her fault he'd felt the need for this late-night walk in the first place. It was Filomena Cromwell who had added this new, unsettling restlessness to his life. The elf should be made to take responsibility for her actions.

But not tonight. Tonight he would allow her to disappear back to the safety of her bedroom or her mushroom castle or wherever it was she vanished to at night. There was no need to rush, Trent told himself as he faded into the shadows. Time was running out for his elfin lady. Soon she would discover that no matter how swiftly she danced or how adroitly she sidestepped, she couldn't escape him.

One of these days Filomena Cromwell would be his.

Trent smiled at the rash promise he had made to himself. All he had to do, he thought, was get her attention. It wasn't as simple as it sounded.

1

FILOMENA CROMWELL WAS HAVING a very good time. The music was enthusiastically played, even if it was being provided by a small-town band. The Gallant Lake Country Club restaurant was filled to capacity with locals out for an evening of dining and dancing. True, the food and the atmosphere were a far cry from New York, San Francisco or Seattle, but Filomena found it deliciously amusing to know that every eye in the room was upon her and the man with whom she was dancing.

She tipped back her head, aware that her long red hair was falling intimately over Trent Ravinder's arm as he held her close. As usual when she danced with a man as big as Ravinder, she was having to exert an unrelenting amount of physical resistance in order to keep from being pulled even closer in his grasp. Large men always tended to overwhelm a woman as short and slender as she was.

But she was accustomed to the maneuvering required to survive on a dance floor, and her eyes were alight with mischief as she looked up at him through her lashes.

"I'm glad to see you function well under pressure, Trent," Filomena murmured.

Trent looked down into her face, his striking green gaze hooded and watchful, although his expression was coolly polite. "This is like dancing in a goldfish bowl. If I'd known we were going to attract this much attention, I would have worn my neon tie and spats."

Filomena laughed in delight. "That certainly would have livened up everyone's evening."

"Oh, I don't know," he said thoughtfully, running a critical eye over her gown. "I have a hunch it would have taken more than a neon tie to compete with that dress you've got on." His hand moved on her back, his fingers warm and deliberate on the shoulder-to-waist triangle of feminine skin exposed by the outfit.

Filomena frowned in mocking concern. "You don't like the dress? I'm crushed. It was designed by my partner. Glenna always knows what looks good on me. I've learned to trust her implicitly when it comes to my clothing."

"Is that right?" Trent's deep, quiet voice sounded unruffled, but there was a distinct note of challenge in it.

"Oh, yes. Glenna always knows what she's doing when it comes to dressing me. She's the one with the talent for design in our firm. My instincts are for fabric and color. We make a good team."

Filomena smiled to herself as Ravinder gave the dark green dress another assessing glance. She knew the gown was one of Glenna Sterling's brilliant combinations of the demure and the disconcerting. The clinging jersey was beautifully fitted to her slender frame, hugging every soft curve. Long sleeves and a high neckline provided an illusion of discreet reserve in front, which was instantly shattered by the daring plunge to the waist in back. The flowing fabric fell into a long sarong skirt that moved beautifully around her legs. The expanse of skin exposed along the length of Filomena's spine left the viewer with the strong conviction she was not wearing a bra. The conviction was correct.

"My congratulations to your partner. She knows how to dress you in a way that makes a man want to undress you. That's a hell of a talent, I suppose, in the fashion business."

Filomena grinned. "Why, Trent. You sound disapproving. More than disapproving. One might almost say prudish. Priggish even? Or puritanical? Downright Victorian, perhaps? I'm left wondering why you asked me to dance?"

"You know damn well why I asked you to dance."

Filomena's grin became a throaty laugh. "Of course I do. I shouldn't tease you about it. I know you're trying to do my family a favor, and it's very generous of you. Not every man would volunteer to try to keep me occupied and out of trouble this evening."

"You think that's why I asked you to dance? I'm doing your family a favor?"

"Certainly." Filomena nodded with absolute conviction. "It's been obvious since I arrived two weeks ago that they're all scared to death I'm going to embarrass them beyond recovery and thus ruin my sister's wedding, not to mention the family's social standing here in Gallant Lake. But there you were staying conveniently at the lodge for most of the summer. My mother took one look at you and decided you were going to be the family's salvation. They're hoping you'll keep me out of mischief at least until after the wedding. Actually I think half the town is waiting to see if you can do it. The other half hopes you'll fail, naturally. The gossip of a really big scandal would be wonderful. Gallant Lake is such a quiet little town most of the time."

Trent studied her vivid gaze for a long moment before he spoke. "You're certainly doing your best to put on a show for the hometown crowd, aren't you? It's been one staged event after another since you arrived, starting with that high-school-prom replay you put on last week."

"That was the prom I never went to," Filomena explained. "I wound up baby-sitting on prom night because I didn't have a date. Hardly a surprise, given the fact that I didn't have a date all during high school. Actually I'm glad I waited ten years for the big event. I'm sure I had a much better time last week than I would have had ten years ago."

"You caused quite a stir when you wrote 'no ex-cheerleaders or football players allowed' on the invitations. Your mother nearly fainted when she got hold of one and read it. She was sure you managed to alienate some very important people in town."

"I wanted this prom to be for those of us who were always on the outside looking in during our high-school years. We had a great time the other night. Spent the evening admiring one another for having proven there is life after high school. Most of us have been quite successful."

"Most of Gallant Lake talked about the party all last week, your mother tells me. Your father says you spent a fortune on champagne and caviar and all the trimmings."

"What's the point of replaying your high-school prom if you don't do it up right? Besides," Filomena added carelessly, "I can afford it."

"You don't mind being the subject of all that speculation and gossip?"

"Not this time," Filomena assured him.

"What do you mean by that?"

"I mean that the last time I gave the town something to talk about, everyone felt sorry for me. I was an object of pity and the subject of a great many I-told-you-sos."

"I find that hard to believe. When was that?"

"Oh, a long time ago," Filomena said smoothly. "Nine years ago to be exact."

"That would have been when you were nineteen?"

"Umm. Some women are quite sophisticated and mature at nineteen. I, unfortunately, was a late bloomer. I was also rather plump, dowdy and not terribly good at making scintillating conversation with a man."

Trent smiled faintly. "I can't imagine you at a loss for words. What happened to bring about the flowering of Filomena Cromwell?"

"Getting away from Gallant Lake helped immeasurably. I shed some pounds that first year in college and began to learn some social graces. It wasn't a big change, not at first, but it was enough to attract the interest of someone back here in Gallant Lake. We started seeing each other when I came home on weekends and vacations. He was a few years older, sophisticated, suave, handsome and all the rest. I was terribly flattered. By spring of that first year in college, I was actually engaged. I couldn't believe it. Some man actually wanted me. *Me*, Filomena Cromwell." Filomena shook her head, smiling indulgently at the memory of the naive young woman she had once been.

"I get the feeling there's a punch line coming."

Filomena shrugged. "No punch line. The remainder of the growing-up process was completed for me in a hurry one day when I found my fiancé in bed with another woman. Someone who had been in my graduating class. One of the in crowd." She smiled. "I'm sure you can imagine my surprise. Everyone in town heard about it within twenty-four hours. My fiancé broke the engagement and told everyone he planned to marry the other woman, that it was her he had loved all along. I, apparently, had just been a way of passing time and I had totally misunderstood his intentions. I wondered at the time if I would survive the humiliation. You know how it is when you're only nineteen."

But Trent Ravinder wasn't smiling. He was still watching her intently. "It must have been quite a shock for a gentle, insecure young woman. Mind telling me who the fiancé was?"

"Don't you know?" Filomena was honestly surprised. "How unfair of my family to assign you the duty of keeping me out of trouble without telling you the exact nature of the problem. It's no secret, believe me. His name is Brady Paxton. He's here with his wife tonight. They're sitting right over there."

She turned her head and looked directly at a big tawny-haired man sitting at a table across the room. The man had been watching her as she danced, and his gaze collided awkwardly with hers when she glanced in his direction. Paxton turned away quickly, but not before Filomena caught the hint of embarrassment in his expression. She smiled to herself.

Ravinder sucked in his breath, his hand tightening with unexpected fierceness around Filomena's waist. "You little witch," he muttered. "He's fascinated with you, isn't he? And you're getting a kick out of putting on a show for the town."

Filomena shook her head, and her smile faded. "No, I'm not particularly enjoying it, but everyone else is certainly excited. It's been like this since I arrived. I gather Brady and his wife are having domestic problems and everyone knows it. It's impossible to keep secrets in a small town. I've been away a long time, and I'm a little out of touch with local events. During the past few years, I've just been home for short visits at Christmas and the occasional weekend. Not long enough to even run into

Brady, let alone seduce him. But now I'm here on the first long vacation I've had in nine years. And I look somewhat different than I did when I left under a cloud of humiliation at the age of nineteen."

"It isn't just your looks that have changed, is it?" Trent asked shrewdly. "In fact, that's probably the least of it. You've also got style and a considerable amount of financial success. Your folks tell me you're doing very well in the fashion business. You've lived in San Francisco and New York learning the trade and now you've got your own sportswear design firm in Seattle. Your dad said that for the past couple of years you've traveled all over the world looking for exotic fabric and design ideas and setting up business contacts. He said your little company, what's it called? Cromwell & Sterling? had a small fortune in orders last year. He said you'd probably double that this year."

Filomena laughed. "I'm afraid that doesn't make me or Glenna self-made millionaires. At least not yet. If you know anything about the apparel business, you know that most of the profits have to be channeled right back into the operation."

"That's true of most young firms," Trent said seriously. "But I get the feeling there's still a fair chunk of change left over for you to play with, isn't there? The entertaining you've been doing here in Gallant Lake has been first-class all the way. That flashy green Porsche you arrived in didn't come cheap, and those earrings you're wearing tonight aren't made of plastic."

"What good is success if you can't enjoy it a little?" Filomena responded.

"So now you've got everything you didn't have nine years ago," Trent observed, sizing up the situation. "Style, polish and money. You've come back to the old hometown to show it all off. And the old flame, now married and apparently feeling restless, is gnawing on his own insides wondering what he's missed. No wonder your family is worried. That's a recipe for disaster."

Filomena considered that. "I'm not so sure," she finally said. "I know that's what everyone thinks, but I learned a lot about Brady nine years ago and I'm here to tell you that he's a businessman first, last and always. It's amusing, I'll admit, to imagine him drooling over what he threw away all those years ago, but I have a hunch there's something more involved."

"Such as?" Trent asked bluntly.

"Such as you," she returned sweetly. "I'm not the only one giving the gossips a field day here in Gallant Lake, Trent. You're doing an equally good job. You must know as well as I do that no one believes for a moment that you're spending six weeks in the Oregon woods just to do some fishing."

Trent smiled slowly, but there was a hard edge to the curve of his mouth. "It's the truth. I'm here on vacation."

"But everyone is convinced that's just camouflage. They think you're here to scout the territory for your development firm. It's called Asgard Development, isn't it? Take a look at all the people sneaking little glances at us. They just know you're going to end up buying a big piece of land near the lake and put in a multimillion-dollar resort. They're all trying to figure out how they can get rich off the deal, Brady Paxton included."

"If you think it's me he's eyeing tonight, you're out of your redheaded brain. He's salivating over you. As for the other angle, I give you my word, I'm here on vacation."

"Whatever you say," Filomena assured him, her eyes gleaming with amusement. "You're entitled to a little business privacy. Believe me, I'd be the last one to deny you that. We keep all kinds of secrets in the fashion-design business."

"You don't believe me?" Trent asked roughly. There was no answering amusement in his green eyes.

"Why should I?"

"Because," he stated with a cool arrogance that was amazingly intimidating, "when I tell you something, you can believe it. I don't lie, Filomena, and I don't tolerate anyone lying to me. I might not talk about a certain matter for a variety of reasons, but I sure as hell wouldn't lie about it. That's something you had better understand up front."

Filomena's eyes widened in astonishment. It seemed to her he was overreacting to a very casual, teasing comment. "Good grief, I didn't mean to insult you. I'm sure you're as honest as the average businessman."

"I'm honest, period. And I expect the people I deal with to return that honesty with interest."

"Or what?" Filomena couldn't resist the soft, goading taunt.

"Do you really want to know?"

She blinked, assimilating the blunt warning. It was obvious she had strayed into dangerous territory. "No, I don't suppose I do. I take it you believe in revenge as much as you believe in being trustworthy? Your word is your bond and everyone else had better prove just as reliable or you'll hound him or her to the ends of the earth? Have I got that straight?"

Trent inclined his head with an arrogant motion. "You seem to have grasped the essentials."

"Why?" Filomena asked softly.

It was Trent's turn to blink. "Why what?"

"Why should I take you totally on trust? Why should I or anyone else believe you?"

Trent looked down into her face. "Because I say so."

"That's supposed to be enough to satisfy me? I should trust you completely just because you say so?"

"You take me on trust, Filomena, or you don't take me at all."

His words sent a chill down her spine. "Well, at least you've allowed me some choice in the matter," she retorted dryly. "I'm relieved to know I have the option of not taking you at all. If you'll excuse me, the dance seems to be over."

She stepped back in a firm bid to break his grip. For an instant nothing happened. Trent didn't release her, and Filomena realized she couldn't escape until he voluntarily let her go. She could feel the easy, unconscious strength in his arm as he held her close, and it disturbed her.

"Scared?" Trent asked softly.

"Not in the least. Just annoyed. Large men always seem to take advantage of their size when they deal with someone smaller than themselves."

"I didn't mean to frighten you," Trent said earnestly as he ignored her subtle efforts to free herself. "I just wanted to get things clear between us."

"The only thing that's clear is that we're the last two people on the dance floor. Whoever might not have been staring at us earlier is certainly doing so now."

That got his attention. He glanced around at the sea of interested faces and scowled. Without further comment he took Filomena's arm and led her off the floor. Filomena's sense of humor quickly reasserted itself.

"I'm sure my family will thank you for taking the tactful approach. Lecturing me on the subject of truth, honesty and integrity while standing in the middle of a dance floor was probably not on the list of duties they expect you to fulfill."

"You can be a sassy little thing at times, can't you? Typical of the species, I suppose."

"What species?"

"The one that includes elves, pixies, imps and assorted mischief makers." The harshness was fading from his expression as he guided her back to the large table occupied by her family. "No wonder your relatives and most of the town are on pins and needles waiting to see what you'll do."

"I think they're equally interested in seeing what you'll do. You seem to have been assigned responsibility for handling me," Filomena shot back. "But I'll give you full marks for being able to dance in a goldfish bowl. Not everyone could have handled that. Did it bother you?"

Trent gave her a sidelong glance. "I'll admit I like my privacy. Especially when it comes to dealing with you. But I can handle a little heat when it's necessary."

Filomena laughed. "I'll just bet you can. Thank you for the dance, Trent. I enjoyed it. At least until the lecture started."

"My pleasure, Filomena. I feel the experience gives us a sort of common bond, don't you? We've faced the assembled society of Gallant Lake together."

"That's one way of looking at it." Her tone was sardonic.

Filomena studied him out of the corner of her eye as they moved back toward the table. She wasn't the only one studying Trent Ravinder, she knew. She was well aware of the interested gaze of her parents and her Aunt

Agnes and Uncle George as well as her sister Shari's curious glances. Shari's fiancé, Jim Devore, appeared amused by the whole event. But there was a certain respect in his dark eyes as he watched Ravinder lead Filomena back to the family fold.

Trent bore the scrutiny well, but that came as no surprise. Filomena had seen the calm inner fortitude in him the moment they had been introduced almost two weeks ago. He was staying at her parents' lakefront inn, the Gallant Lake Lodge, and right from the start he had apparently become more than just a paying guest. He was rapidly assuming the status of an old friend of the family. It was a clever trick. The Cromwells were gracious hosts, but they rarely adopted their clientele.

Trent Ravinder's inner strength had an outward manifestation. He was a big, lean, broad-shouldered man who moved with a confident, contained vitality. He was over six feet in height, and that made him too tall as far as Filomena was concerned. She was only five feet three inches, and she had an instinctive dislike of being towered over by other people, especially men. The only exception to the rule was her father.

The shards of green jewels that formed Trent's eyes were the most riveting element in a face that was composed of hard ridges and stark planes. Those eyes betrayed a cool intelligence and a fierce will that made it easy to believe he would be successful at whatever he chose to do. But even the brilliance of his gaze couldn't make him a handsome man; there was too much power and too much rough-edged determination in that face to allow room for good looks.

Ravinder's hair was thick and dark with a sprinkling of silver at the temples that made it clear he was well into his thirties. Filomena had automatically assessed his clothing with a knowing eye the day she'd met him. It was immediately obvious that Trent wore his clothes; they didn't wear him.

There was nothing flashy or trendy about his taste. In fact, he appeared to have a decided preference for conservative styles. They suited him. He looked good and was comfortable in everything from the faded jeans he wore during the day to the expensive slacks and jacket he had on tonight. He'd paid good money to get that jacket to fit his hard, massive frame that well, Filomena knew.

All in all, there was no doubt that Trent looked successful and motivated. He didn't look like the kind of man who would take six weeks off in the middle of summer to go fishing in the Oregon woods. It was far more likely he was in town for the business reason everyone assumed.

But he'd claimed he was here only for a vacation and, Filomena reflected with a smile, Trent certainly didn't take to having his word questioned. The arrogance of the man was amusing now that she was no longer dealing with it in the middle of a dance floor.

For a woman who was rather enjoying the stir she was causing in her hometown, she had discovered an alarming dislike of being involved in a public scene with Trent Ravinder. Perhaps that was because she suspected that if push ever came to shove, she probably wouldn't win in any confrontation with the man. Filomena didn't like the feeling. These days she was accustomed to winning.

During the past few years she had learned the pleasures of her own personal strength, determination and abilities. She was not the weak, naive little fool who had once made such an idiot of herself over a man from Gallant Lake, Oregon. Business success, extensive travel and the necessity of working with a variety of top-level creative, often temperamental people had taught her just how much internal power she had. She had an abundance of confidence and poise now. She didn't appreciate the notion that Trent Ravinder, a man she barely knew, could ruffle those hard-won qualities, even for a moment. She had been right to keep him at bay for the past two weeks.

As they approached the table, Trent reluctantly released his hold on Filomena. He smiled at her parents. Filomena had to admit he had certainly charmed them.

"I've brought her back safe and sound."

Amery Cromwell smiled pleasantly. Filomena's father had bequeathed her his red hair and hazel-gold eyes. "Of course you did. What could happen on a dance floor? Sit down, both of you. Agnes and George have ordered some champagne to toast the engaged couple."

"Just the thing for celebrating engagements, I always say," Aunt Agnes declared cheerfully. She was older than her brother, somewhere in her sixties. The deep red hair of former years had long since turned gray, but Agnes refused to accept the inevitable. Agnes also refused to pay the fees charged by professional hairstylists. She bought her own hair-coloring supplies at the local drugstore, and she never quite followed the instructions apparently. Either that or she preferred to exercise a measure of creativity. The result was a halo of short curls dyed a vivid shade of orange.

George Buckner, Agnes's husband, was a self-made man and proud of it. He had put his money into real estate for the past forty years. He loved land and had a deep, abiding faith in it as an investment. He was also a big man, and Filomena and her sister had learned from the cradle that his spirit of generosity was as large as the rest of him.

George and Agnes had never had children of their own, and they had delighted in giving their nieces presents on all major occasions. They would have given Filomena and Shari more down through the years if Amery and Meg Cromwell hadn't taken a firm stand against too many gifts. The parents had been afraid the girls would be spoiled. But George and Agnes had found ways to smuggle small, delightful presents to their nieces at odd moments when everyone thought Amery and Meg weren't looking. Filomena knew Uncle George and Aunt Agnes loved the pleasure of surprising her and her sister.

Trent's gaze swept the family group as he seated Filomena. He noticed that Agnes was sipping at another martini. It was her third. After knowing her for a couple of weeks, he was not surprised.

He smiled at the older woman as he took his own seat beside Filomena. "You surprise me, Agnes. I would have expected you to order a bottle of gin for Shari and Jim, not champagne."

"Never let it be said I don't respect the traditions," Agnes said firmly. "Besides, gin is expressly designed for retired schoolteachers. Young ones such as Shari should still try to get a variety in their diet." She toasted her soon-to-be married niece with her martini glass.

"Too bad not everyone around here has some respect for the traditions," George inserted with a glowering look at Filomena that only barely masked his amusement.

Filomena's expression was innocent. It was something she did well, Trent had decided. It worked because there really was a genuine, fundamental innocence about her that seemed to go hand in hand with the underlying spirit of mischief. She smiled serenely at her uncle. "Are you implying I lack suitable respect for wedding customs and conventions, Uncle George?"

"We've been hearing about that so-called 'ladies' night out' party you gave for Shari night before last."

Shari spoke up. "That was my 'farewell to singlehood' party. Every woman is entitled to one. Men have bachelor parties, don't they?"

"That's not the point," Uncle George declared. He turned to Shari's fiancé. "Have you heard about that party?"

"I've heard," Jim said dryly. "Frankly, the less I hear, the better. I have a feeling this may be one of those cases where ignorance is bliss."

Agnes lowered her voice and glared at Filomena. "Well, out of sight is definitely not out of mind. Not in a town this size. You know what everyone's saying, don't you? Gossip has it that you imported a male stripper along with the wine and canapés. But no one knows for certain because none of the women who attended is talking. I have been told," she concluded ominously, "that a condition for attending the party was a vow of silence. Nothing was more likely to get everyone talking about it, and you know it."

"I would like to take this opportunity to state categorically that I definitely did not import a male stripper for Shari's party," Filomena said piously.

Shari nearly choked on her wine. Jim Devore gave his bride-to-be a severe look.

Trent, who, along with everyone else at the lodge, had heard the laughter that had emanated from behind the sealed doors of the lodge's old ballroom the night of the party, raised quizzical eyebrows at Filomena. Mischief he would tolerate but the elf needed to learn that he wouldn't allow any outright lies. "Is that a fact?"

Filomena lifted her chin, her eyes filled with laughter. "Yes, it's a fact. Damian Fontaine is no sleazy stripper."

"What is he then?" Trent asked politely, remembering the glimpse he had caught of the lean, muscular young man he had seen being smuggled in amid a crowd of caterers who had arrived from a larger, neighboring town.

"Mr. Fontaine bills himself as an exotic dancer," Filomena explained in haughty accents. "He's had classical ballet training, you know."

A groan echoed around the table. Shari had to work to suppress her giggles.

"I should have known the rumors were true," Jim remarked, looking resigned. "Be warned, Trent. The women in this family need a firm hand on the reins."

"Oh, dear," Filomena's mother said in pained tones. "Then it's true, there *was* a stripper at the lodge the other night. How will I ever explain it?"

"He was not a stripper!" Filomena declared staunchly. No one paid any attention to her denial.

Trent gave Meg Cromwell a reassuring look. "My suggestion is that you rise above it and pretend it never happened. Hope and pray that the ladies who attended will keep their vows of secrecy and that the gossip will fade."

"I seem to have done a lot of pretending and hoping and praying in that regard since Filomena showed up a couple of weeks ago."

Trent slanted the older woman a quick, sympathetic grin. He liked Meg. She made an excellent hostess for the Gallant Lake Lodge. There was an air of tranquil relaxation about the place, but under the surface everything was run with efficiency. He had a hunch that underlying efficiency was largely due to Meg Cromwell. Her husband's talents lay in other directions. Amery was a first-rate accountant and fly fisherman. The lodge relied on his skills in both areas.

Aunt Agnes intervened. "I warned you we were going to have to keep an eye on that redheaded gal of yours while she's here. She's in a mood to cause trouble. Just look at that itty-bitty scrap of a dress that shows half her backside. A few years ago Amery would have sent her back upstairs to change if she'd showed up ready to go out to dinner in a dress like that."

Filomena gave her aunt a fond look. "Just be grateful it doesn't show half of my front side, too, Aunt Agnes. I've got another one that does."

Agnes plunked her glass down on the table and gave a shout of laughter. She pointed a bright red fingernail at Trent. "You see what I mean? Nothing but trouble, that gal. Sassy, independent and reckless. You need a husband to look after you, Filomena Cromwell. Someone to keep you in line."

"You know how I feel about marriage, Aunt Agnes."

"You'd change your mind if the right man ever came along." Agnes gave a woeful sigh. "Who'd have thought someone that small could cause so much mischief? Think you can handle her, Trent?"

Trent was aware of Filomena's quelling glance but he chose to ignore it as he answered her aunt. He knew that even though it had been Agnes who had asked the question, that same anxious query was in the minds of the rest of the family. Amusement lit his eyes. Filomena really had them going, he thought. "Trust me, Agnes. I'll keep her out of trouble."

Everyone except Filomena laughed as if he'd made a clever joke, but Ravinder heard the underlying note of relief buried beneath the humor. Filomena said nothing. She sipped her glass of white wine and looked at him over the rim as if he were an alien entity she had accidentally stumbled upon. She was deciding what to do with him, Trent knew. The cool, calculating expression in her hazel-gold eyes told him she hadn't yet figured out just what approach to use. Once she made up her mind, she would be a formidable opponent.

Unless he disarmed her first, Trent thought. *Unless he turned her into a sweet, loving lady who would save all that fire and ice for the bedroom. His bedroom.* He felt himself tighten with an annoying but increasingly familiar rush of desire. He had begun suffering these unexpected bouts of sensual arousal soon after he'd been introduced to Filomena Cromwell, and he was a long way from getting accustomed to them. For years he had been coolly in control of himself in virtually all areas of his life, including his own sexual needs. It was both irritating and exciting to discover that this redheaded slip of a woman had the power to threaten his masculine control.

He glanced at Filomena as the conversation changed to a discussion of the new house Jim and Shari planned to buy. Filomena appeared to be interested in what was being said, but Trent sensed she was still very aware of him. Good. It was some consolation to know that she couldn't dismiss him completely from her mind when something else caught her attention. But her absorption in the topic of house buying gave him a chance to examine her thoughtfully.

As usual she looked like an elfin queen among a flock of handsome giants. That had been Ravinder's first impression of her, and it returned every time he saw her surrounded by her family.

The fact was, Filomena was quite short by Cromwell standards. Even the women in the family were tall. Her mother and her sister and her aunt were all six or seven inches taller than she was and built along Junoesque lines. The men were even larger. Filomena's father and her Uncle George were well over six feet, and there was a sense of solid density about both of them. The newest member of the family, Jim Devore, was built like a football player and probably stood six-one or two.

Filomena was petite, slender and delicate. Trent knew he could cup one of her round, pert breasts easily in the palm of his hand. He could wrap both hands around the enticing swell of her derriere. The knowledge didn't do much to drain the sensual tension from his body.

The slinky gown Filomena was wearing emphasized her narrow waist and the lush, sweet flare of her hips and thighs. She might be diminutive in height, but she was a good object lesson on the wonders of proportion, Trent told himself. For the past two weeks he had known beyond a shadow of a doubt that she would be absolutely perfect for his bed. The thought of her lying beneath him, responding to him was enough to make him work to stifle a groan.

Filomena turned her head at that moment, her gaze locking briefly with his, and Trent knew she had read his thoughts. He saw the faint, betraying flush in her cheeks, and he smiled. He wanted her aware of him. She had been staying out of reach for too long. Her response to his knowing smile was a quick flash of feminine anger in her wide eyes, and then she looked away again, refusing to meet his gaze any longer.

Trent took a sip of his beer and considered Filomena's profile. The red hair flowed in luxurious waves down her back, practically begging a man to twist his hands in its depths and feel the fire. Her large hazel-gold eyes were framed by soft, casually brushed bangs that had obviously been professionally styled to compliment the shape of her face. She was no riveting beauty, but it took quite a while to realize it because her features were so expressive. When a man did realize it, he no longer cared one way or the other about classical beauty. Filomena offered so much more. Laughter, anger, passion—all those expressions came easily to her elfin face.

Trent remembered what she had said about once being plump. It amused him to think of her that way. He was willing to bet he would find Filomena just as sexy with twenty pounds more on her bones as he found her now, and that was very, very sexy, indeed.

Trent considered the role the Cromwell family had more or less assigned him. He knew Filomena's people were worried. Even he had heard the gossip about the Paxtons' domestic problems. He'd seen Gloria Paxton earlier this evening sitting with her husband. It was obvious she had once been a very attractive young woman, but her natural beauty was hidden tonight beneath an expression of resentment and pouting depression. Gloria Paxton was a sad, bitter, discontented woman, and it showed.

Trent had heard Meg Cromwell remark privately that Gloria had put on weight since the birth of her second child. But it need not have affected her attractiveness, Trent decided, if she had dressed to suit her changed figure. Unfortunately it was obvious Gloria Paxton was still trying to pretend she was a size eight. The result was that she looked as if she'd been poured into the silver lamé dress she was wearing, her large breasts threatening to spill out of the front while the seams around the hipline appeared ready to burst. The skirt was much too short. Nothing seemed in proper proportion.

Gloria's hair was an unnatural shade of platinum blond, stiff with lacquer and done in a wild, flamboyant style that seemed all wrong for her face. It was a style that might have looked cute on a coed a decade ago. On top of everything else, Gloria's makeup was far too heavy.

All in all, Trent decided, he felt sorry for Gloria Paxton. It was hard to imagine her as the woman who had stolen away Filomena's fiancé nine years before.

Trent's sympathy for the Paxtons ended there. Every time he caught a glimpse of Brady Paxton he felt nothing but a cold need to assert himself and make it clear that Paxton no longer had any rights at all to Filomena Cromwell.

Because in spite of what Filomena had said on the dance floor, Trent was certain of what he had seen in Paxton's gaze when the other man had looked at Filomena. There was no doubt that Paxton wanted another shot at the woman he had once rejected. The man had hardly been able to take his eyes off Filomena all evening. The humble daisy of yesterday had bloomed into a brilliant, exotic flower, and Paxton wanted to pluck it.

Which, of course, was precisely why Trent Ravinder had been drafted into the role of escort for Filomena. The last thing the Cromwells wanted was a scandal on the eve of Shari Cromwell's wedding. Filomena could go back to Seattle after it was all over and laugh to her heart's content; the rest of the Cromwells would have to stay in town and endure the aftermath.

Filomena Cromwell was, in the eyes of her family and most of the neighbors, a wild card, unpredictable and potentially dangerous.

Trent found himself smiling in anticipation.

2

FILOMENA STAYED on her best behavior for the remainder of the evening. She was well aware that Trent Ravinder was poised like a hunting cat, waiting for her to put a foot wrong. It amused her to wonder what he thought he could actually do if she did decide to cause trouble.

She was warmly polite to all the people who came by the table to congratulate Shari and Jim and say hello to her. She chatted briefly with several old acquaintances with whom she had once gone to school. Many of them couldn't help sneaking amazed glances at her. Obviously Brady Paxton wasn't the only one who seemed to be wondering what had happened to the previous version of Filomena Cromwell.

But the evening didn't get really exciting until Gloria and Brady Paxton left their table and started toward the Cromwells. Even from this distance it was easy to see the idea of saying hello was not Gloria's. It would be the first time Filomena had confronted Brady and Gloria in person since her return. She heard her sister's quick intake of breath as the Paxtons made their way across the crowded room. Then she saw Jim reach over to pat his fiancée's hand reassuringly. Meg Cromwell shot Filomena a quelling glance. Amery eyed his daughter warily. Aunt Agnes and Uncle George had the same expressions they always got just before the fireworks started at the town's annual Fourth of July celebration.

Trent didn't move, but he picked up his glass of beer and smiled deliberately and dangerously at Filomena.

Filomena had to struggle to keep from laughing. She thought of telling everyone not to worry, that the last thing she wanted was Brady Paxton back, but then she asked herself why she should spoil the fun. The rest of the family and half the diners in the room were obviously suffering that delightful sense of terror and anxiety one experienced at the top of a roller coaster.

Instead of offering reassurance to her nervous relatives, Filomena took the opportunity to examine Brady Paxton in detail. No doubt about it, she must have been a fool nine years ago. She really couldn't imagine what she had ever seen in him. As she looked at him, she realized she felt absolutely nothing except regret at having wasted her freshman year in college pining for him.

Brady had played football in high school, but now he had a distinct businessman's bulge at the waistline. Too much time spent behind a desk and not enough at the gym, Filomena decided. The additional weight was minor, however. It wasn't sufficient to detract much from his open, outdoorsy good looks.

He still had those blue bedroom eyes and that wealth of tawny-brown hair. Dressed in a properly fitting jacket he would always be a handsome man by most standards, but Filomena thought he looked oddly soft and uninteresting to her now. She hadn't noticed it when she'd been on the verge of turning twenty, but now she realized what was missing in Brady. There was no sense of depth to him, nothing that demanded respect or promised emotional strength when it was needed.

It was then Filomena acknowledged to herself that those were precisely the qualities she had sensed in Trent Ravinder. There was a steel core in Trent that was totally lacking in Paxton. She knew instinctively, and with a certainty she couldn't explain, that while Ravinder might be arrogant, demanding, stubborn and difficult at times, he would also be a rock when he was needed.

Fortunately, she thought, she didn't need any rocks in her life.

"Good evening, Amery, Meg..." Brady Paxton greeted everyone politely until he'd made the rounds of the table. Amery introduced him to Ravinder, explaining that Trent was staying at the lodge for the summer. The two men exchanged short, stiff nods. Brady's eyes kept returning to Filomena, who smiled her most dazzling smile in response. "Good to see you again, Fil. It's been a long time."

Aware of the hostility in Gloria's eyes, Filomena sorted through several rejoinders and finally came up with the blandest one she could find. "Yes, hasn't it? Time flies when you're having fun. How's the insurance business?" Brady had joined Gloria's father's insurance agency shortly after marrying Gloria. The agency's name had promptly been changed from Halsey Insurance to Halsey-Paxton Insurance. At the time, that had seemed more important than anything else in the world to Brady.

Brady nodded complacently. "Can't complain. We hear you're doing very well, Fil. Quite the little entrepreneur, huh?"

Gloria spoke up. "Yes, Fil, we hear you're involved in the fashion business. Lots of travel and shows and wheeling and dealing. Who would have guessed you had any talent in that direction?"

Filomena turned up the voltage of her smile. "I certainly didn't show much flair for it in high school, did I? But that was because I hadn't had any training in the principles of design. I've always loved color and fabric and style. I just didn't understand them or how they applied to someone my size when I was a girl."

Gloria's expression soured at the good-natured response. "That's right, you concentrate on styles for short women, don't you? Nothing I'd be interested in."

"That's correct. My firm designs exclusively for petite women," Filomena murmured, remembering how she had once envied Gloria's five feet seven inches of model-perfect figure. "Officially the term refers to women five foot four and under. There are millions of women who aren't tall enough to look really good in the standard sizes."

"I know," Gloria said with an acid pity. "Poor things. They tend to look swamped in their clothes, regardless of how much they pay for them. Sleeves are too long, waistlines don't fit right, hem lengths are dowdy-looking. Must be very depressing."

Out of the corner of her eye, Filomena saw Shari bite her lip. Filomena had once looked that way in her own clothing, and everyone knew it. Her plumpness at the time hadn't helped. She knew her sister was about to jump to her defense, even if it did mean creating the scene the family had hoped to avoid. Filomena kicked her sister under the table in an old warning left over from childhood. Shari frowned but swallowed whatever it was she had been about to say.

"It's all a matter of proportion, Gloria, as I'm sure you realize," Filomena said easily, determined to defuse the situation. She had no quarrel with Gloria Paxton. If anything she felt sorry for her. "The right fit in clothes makes all the difference."

"Well, your clothes have certainly made a difference in you," Gloria observed coldly. The implication was clear. Gloria was attributing all of Filomena's obvious success and style to her clothes alone.

Filomena's eyes danced as she thought of the years of hard work, tension and penny-pinching anxiety behind her. The clothes she now wore were the least important change that had occurred in her life. Her laughter bubbled forth, warm and genuine. She picked up her wineglass.

"Thank you for noticing, Gloria. I realize I've changed during the past few years. Lucky for me, hmm? I don't even want to think about what a disaster it would have been for me to have married and settled down when I was nineteen. It's so easy to make foolish mistakes at that age, isn't it?" She grinned. "Just think of what I would have been like if I'd stayed here in Gallant Lake. No style, no Porsche, no travel, no fun at all. A woman sometimes needs time to come into her own."

There was a moment's silence around the table as everyone absorbed the underlying fact that Gloria Paxton probably thought she had been the one who had made the mistake when she was nineteen. Gloria's face turned a dull red.

Shari and her mother made a few frantic but false conversational starts in an effort to smooth over the awkward situation, but it was Amery who coughed and looked determinedly at Brady.

"Say, I think my fire insurance policy is about due for renewal, isn't it, Brady? Let me know if I need to update the coverage. Can't afford to be without decent insurance in my business, you know."

"I'll review the policy for you, Amery," Brady said absently. He seemed unaware of his wife's hostility. He switched his attention to Trent. "How are you enjoying your summer on the lake, Ravinder?"

Trent smiled meaningfully at Filomena. "I don't think it's going to be boring."

Filomena sensed the cool claim Trent was making and knew it had not gone unnoticed by Brady or anyone else. She didn't like it, but there wasn't much she could do about it at that moment. Brady frowned. "I hear you work for Asgard Development."

"That's right."

"They've been doing a lot of resort development in Arizona and Hawaii for the past few years."

"Resort development is Asgard's specialty." Trent's voice was strictly neutral.

Brady summoned up his best business smile. "Local gossip says Asgard has sent you here to look us over."

"Is that right? Well, you know what they say about gossip," Trent said casually.

"I know what they say about smoke," Brady shot back bluntly.

Trent looked at him. "If I were you, I wouldn't waste any time looking for the fire. Not in this case. I'm here for a vacation, not business."

Brady chuckled and held up a hand. "Say no more. I get the picture. In your business I know you have to watch your tongue. But if I can be of any help in familiarizing you with the area, just let me know. I've lived here all my life, and I've got a lot of contacts. I know everyone who's anyone in business around this neck of the woods. Done some real estate investment myself, you know. I've got a feel for the area."

"Thank you," Trent said with grave politeness. "I'll keep that in mind."

Brady turned back to Filomena. "Hey, little buddy, we'll have to get together while you're in town. Catch up on old times. We've got a lot to talk about, you and I.

Have you told Trent that we were once engaged?" Behind him, Gloria looked more resentful than ever.

Filomena was about to gently deny that she had anything to talk about with Brady, but she never got the chance. Trent stepped in to answer before Filomena could speak.

"I'm afraid Filomena's going to be very busy while she's here. And, yes, she's mentioned the engagement. As she said, it's easy to make mistakes when you're nineteen. But she seems to know her own mind now. She and I are discovering we have a lot in common."

"Oh, ho," Brady said, undaunted. A sly expression crossed his face. "So that's the way it is, huh?" He winked broadly at Filomena. "Never a dull moment for you these days, right?"

"Right." Filomena shot Trent a dark glance. "A few highly exasperating moments, but seldom any dull ones."

Trent smiled with arrogant complacency. "I aim to please."

Filomena gritted her teeth behind her sugary smile. "The question, of course, is how good is your aim?"

"Practice makes perfect. When I take you home tonight, I'll try to get in a little more practice. I'm sure I'll get it right one of these days."

Aunt Agnes nearly choked on her own giggles. Filomena felt herself turning a vivid pink as her aunt led everyone else at the table in a roar of delighted laughter. Brady Paxton tried for an amused expression, but it turned slightly sour. Gloria just glared at Filomena. The Paxtons excused themselves while the laughter still filled the air around the Cromwell table.

Filomena contented herself by giving Trent a cool, dismissing look. The man was going to prove difficult, it seemed. Well, two could play at that game. She smiled at him with cold challenge.

"I'm sure your qualifications are excellent when it comes to developing multimillion-dollar resorts, Trent, but I think this other job you seem to be trying to undertake is a little outside your area of expertise. I wouldn't want to see you bite off more than you can chew."

He grinned at her. "Don't worry about me, Filomena. I've got staying power."

Aunt Agnes toasted him with her martini glass. "You listen to him, gal. Lot to be said for staying power in a man. The Brady Paxtons of this world haven't got it. I should know. Had that Paxton boy in my sixth-grade class. I knew the day you got engaged to him you'd made a big mistake. Didn't George and I tell you so? Damn glad to see it end, I can tell you."

"Now, Agnes," George interrupted, "there's no need to go over that old business."

"That's right," Meg decreed smoothly. She gave Filomena a direct look. "That's all in the past. I'm sure Filomena has no intention of raking over old ashes, do you, Fil?"

"Who, me?"

Shari gave her sister a perceptive glance. "Filomena would have to be out of her mind to want Paxton back, but you couldn't really blame her if she decided to exact a bit of revenge while she's here. I mean, it wouldn't be hard. It's as plain as the nose on his face that Brady is drooling already. And poor Gloria is an easy target."

"It would be like shooting fish in a barrel," Trent stated bluntly. "Which is one very good reason why Filomena isn't going to bother with revenge. It would be too easy, and she doesn't need it."

Filomena leaned back in her chair and toyed with her wineglass. The man was really beginning to annoy her. "How would you know what I need, Trent?"

Amery coughed loudly. "Uh, it's getting late, isn't it? Got to be up early tomorrow morning if we want to get in some good fishing, Trent. Meg, Agnes, George, come on, let's head for home. Shari and Jim probably want to stay and dance a while longer, but the rest of us need our beauty sleep."

Filomena laughed at her father as he made a production out of the departure. "Trying to get me out of public view, Dad? Relax. I'm having a good time. I think I'll stay here with Shari and Jim. They won't mind."

"Of course we won't mind," Jim Devore said gallantly. "We'll take you home, Fil."

But Trent was already on his feet. "Amery's right. It's time for the rest of us to leave, and that includes the potential troublemaker in the crowd. Come along, Filomena. I'll drive you back to the lodge."

"Thanks, but no thanks." Filomena made no move to get to her feet along with everyone else. "I think I'd like to dance some more."

"Is that right?" Trent put a hand on her shoulder as she sat firmly in her chair. "Just who are you planning to dance with?"

"Oh, there's a whole roomful of people here tonight, see?" She waved a blithe hand at the crowd around them. "I'm sure there must be someone my height in here. What about Derek Overton, Shari? He was only about five-six or seven. The perfect size for me. Is he still in town?"

Shari grinned. "Afraid not. Derek announced he was gay, became a lawyer and moved to Portland a few years ago."

"Ah, well, there must be someone else." Filomena wriggled her fingers in a goodbye gesture at Trent. "Run along, Trent. I'll be just fine. I'm very good at taking care of myself these days, in spite of what my family thinks."

Trent responded by putting both of his large, strong hands on her shoulders. He lifted her to her feet as easily as if she were made of feathers. "I'm not so fortunate. I have the distinct feeling I might get lost on the way back to the lodge tonight if I don't have you along as a navigator. Say good night, Filomena."

Aware that her family was watching anxiously and that several people at nearby tables were displaying an open, avid curiosity, Filomena decided to give in gracefully. She really had no desire to cause a scene that would embarrass everyone concerned.

"Good night, Shari, Jim. Enjoy yourselves. Wish I could do the same." Filomena knew Shari and Jim could barely contain their amusement as she was led away.

"Don't try to sound so pathetic and woebegone," Trent advised as he prodded her toward the door. Amery was already shepherding the rest of the family through the crowd. "It doesn't work. Somehow it's tough to summon up a lot of sympathy for you tonight. You've been having a great time terrorizing everyone, haven't you?"

"I don't know why everyone insists on thinking I'm here to make trouble," Filomena complained. "I'm in town for a well-earned vacation and my sister's wedding. That's all."

"Uh-huh. You're swimming through these waters like a sleek, little barracuda, trying to look harmless and innocent."

"I am harmless and innocent."

"The hell you are. I saw that gleam in your eye when the Paxtons came over to the table."

"You said yourself that trying for revenge against those two would be like shooting fish in a barrel. You were right. And if you're fair, you'll admit I behaved myself very well tonight."

Trent's mouth curved faintly. "Okay, I'll admit you managed to resist a few of the obvious temptations that were put in your path. You didn't flirt with Paxton and you didn't get too nasty with his wife, although it was close there for a while."

"I was provoked."

"True." He pushed open the glass doors and ushered her outside into the velvet darkness of an Oregon summer night. "But I can't help wondering how far things would have gone if the rest of us hadn't been around to pull on the reins."

"Not far." Filomena waved to her father who had just finished helping her mother into the family car. "Baiting Paxton would have gotten very boring very quickly, I think. Who wants to be bored?"

"I'll try not to bore you, Filomena," Trent said coolly as he opened the door of his gray Mercedes and put her into the front seat. He shut the door deliberately on her answering comment.

Filomena glared at him through the windshield as he came around the front of the car, but by the time he was sliding into the seat beside her, she had stopped glaring. She was suddenly aware of just how much space he seemed to occupy in the vehicle. He really was a big man. Automatically she edged a little closer into her own corner as she fastened the seat belt. She watched Trent shrug out of his expensive jacket and toss it carelessly onto the back seat. "This whole thing is really very funny, isn't it?"

Trent switched on the ignition and put his arm along the back of the seat as he glanced over his shoulder. He backed the Mercedes neatly out of its slot in the parking lot. "You seem to find it all amusing. If you thought it was going to be fun to return to the old hometown and show everyone how much you've changed, why haven't you done it before now?"

Filomena shrugged. "There hasn't been much opportunity. I haven't gotten where I am by taking vacations. This is my first real one in ages. Usually I just grab a weekend here and there, and frankly there are more exciting places to spend a weekend than Gallant Lake. You're in a high-pressure business. You must know how it is."

"I know," he said with unexpected empathy. He guided the car out onto the narrow road that led back along the lake toward the lodge. "Sometimes we need to slow down and take the time to sort out priorities. I'm here on vacation, too, remember?"

"That's not what Brady Paxton thinks."

"I'm not interested in what Paxton thinks. I'm interested in what you think."

"Is that right?" She slanted him a covert glance. His face looked hard and unyielding in the shadowed confines of the car. But that didn't surprise her. Trent's face looked hard and unyielding most of the time except when he flashed his brief rather wicked smiles. "Why would you care what I think, Trent?"

"Seriously?"

She nodded. "Seriously. I know that you were doing my family a favor tonight by acting as an escort for me, but I figure that's about all it amounts to—a favor. Why should you care what I think about you?"

"If you have to ask that, then you haven't learned as much as you think you have during the past few years. Maybe we should talk about the gap in your education."

Before Filomena could answer, he slowed the car unexpectedly, turning off onto a tiny side road that led down to the lakefront.

Filomena straightened in her seat, her curiosity and desire to bait Trent fading rapidly as a new kind of tension rippled through her. "Where are we going, Trent?"

"To the fishing spot your father took me to yesterday morning." He reduced his speed even more to compensate for the unpaved surface. The narrow track wound down toward the lake through a thick stand of pine and fir.

Filomena told herself she ought to make a firm and forceful protest before they reached the water's edge. She was almost positive Trent would turn back if she made a fuss. He was, after all, a friend of the family. Her father certainly liked and trusted him, and Trent appeared to return the respect Amery showed him. Such a man would not abuse that trust. If she demanded to be driven straight home, Trent would do it. Filomena was sure of it.

Perhaps it was because she was so certain of it that she she refrained from making the demand. Trent probably intended to kiss her, but that hardly constituted an earthshaking event. She could handle him.

Filomena relaxed in her seat as Trent brought the Mercedes to a halt at the edge of the lake. He turned off the engine and rolled down his window. The whisper of the wind in the treetops made its way into the car. Moonlight glittered faintly on the surface of the dark lake. On the far side an occasional pinpoint of light marked the location of a house or a car driving along the shore. The evidence of human habitation was sparse and distant, however. Filomena was suddenly aware of how very much alone she and Trent were.

Trent unfastened his seat belt and turned slightly, draping one arm over the wheel as he lounged back into his corner. He definitely filled up more than his fair share of the car, Filomena thought. And she couldn't help noticing the faint gleam in his gaze.

"We made a good catch here just at dawn yesterday," Trent murmured. "The lake was like glass, and you could see every tiny ripple the fish made. Watching you is a similar experience. Did you know that? You've got a smooth, glossy surface, but it's easily disturbed by whatever emotion you're feeling. I like that. The laughter moves through your eyes and across your mouth the way the ripples move on the lake. So do irritation and sympathy and friendliness and anger."

"Did you bring me here to tell me I'm easy to read?"

"No." He reached over and unbuckled her seat belt. "I brought you here to see if passion moves through you the way all your other emotions do. I want to see if I can feel the ripples."

Filomena tensed as she found herself being enfolded in Trent's arms, her soft, slender frame cradled against his hard body. She felt the heat in him and inhaled the faint tang of soap and after-shave and an indefinable male essence that threatened to swamp her senses.

"So you're running an experiment on me, is that it?" she asked.

"Call it what you want." He looked down into her face as his hand moved through her hair and found the triangle of flesh exposed by the deep V in the back of the gown.

Filomena shivered a little as his warm fingers made contact with her bare skin. "Just remember you're not the only one who can run an experiment."

He traced the graceful line of her spine with a blunt-tipped finger. "I'll share the results I get with you if you'll share the results you get with me."

Filomena was torn between a deep, sensual curiosity and an abrupt burst of uncertainty. She wasn't really afraid of Trent, but she was suddenly afraid of the situation. For two weeks she had adroitly managed to prevent anything from occurring. Now the decision had been taken out of her hands. This wasn't going to be just a casual experiment, and she knew it. Her nervousness, she realized, stemmed from the fact that she was fairly certain Trent knew it, too.

But it was too late to call a halt now. Filomena felt both trapped and oddly comforted in the strong arms that were holding her. Her hands moved upward to brace herself against Trent's broad shoulders. She lifted her face to find the truth in his eyes, but his mouth came down on hers before she could see anything clearly.

Filomena's coral-colored nails sank reflexively into the fabric of Trent's white shirt, biting into the hard, muscled skin underneath as she endured the first impact of his kiss. Somehow, she thought dazedly, it just wasn't what she had been expecting. But she also realized she couldn't have described just exactly what she had been expecting.

Perhaps she had been anticipating more of a tentative, exploratory approach. Perhaps she had assumed there would be a little more initial hesitation. She should have known better, she told herself.

She should have realized that with this man everything would be deliberate, bold and inevitable. She ought to have expected this heat and this fierce, unleashed demand. He was not the kind of man who would do anything in a halfhearted or hesitant way. Most especially he would not make love to a woman with anything other than full power.

Trent's kiss was a deep, ravening thing that engulfed Filomena even as it compelled her response. Her mouth opened of its own volition, granting him an even more intimate access. When she felt the probing touch of his tongue, she shuddered.

Trent's response was a groan of hungry desire that she could feel deep in his chest. His hand moved across her bare shoulders to the narrow sleeve of her dress. "I knew it," he muttered against her mouth. "I knew I'd be able to feel the ripples go through you."

"Trent . . ."

But his fingers were already sliding beneath the fabric of her dress at the shoulders. With a smooth, easy movement, he tugged the front of the gown downward, sliding the jersey sleeves to her wrists and the once demure neckline almost to her waist.

Filomena gasped in startled dismay. It had happened too quickly, leaving her exposed and vulnerable long before she had made the decision herself. She pulled back but discovered she was bound, her hands trapped in her dress sleeves. Her widening eyes flew to his.

"Take it easy, honey. You know I'm not going to hurt you." Trent caught her wrists and began easing her hands free. His eyes roved over her bared breasts, and just before he released her wrists, he bent his head to drop a featherlight kiss on one budding nipple.

Another shiver of desire went through Filomena. Nervous tension followed in its wake. "Trent, this has gone far enough," she began in a soft, throaty voice that she knew betrayed her clouded emotions.

"I just want to touch you."

His tone was heavy with desire, but Filomena could feel the control he had on himself. She was as safe as she wanted to be. The knowledge only added to the sensation of walking a high wire. When his fingertips cupped her small, rounded breasts and grazed lightly across the nipples, she moaned.

And then her hands were free, and instead of pushing herself away and recovering her dress, Filomena found herself clinging to Trent. She buried her hot face against his shoulder and closed her eyes as excitement rippled through her.

"I knew it would be like this," Trent whispered roughly. "Ever since you arrived two weeks ago, I've known. Every time I've looked at you, I've ached because I realized what it would be like. I don't know how I waited this long."

"Oh, Trent . . ."

"Hush. Just relax and let it happen. It's going to happen, you know."

"Not tonight."

"If not tonight, then another night. It might as well be now."

Desperately she struggled to resist the compelling quality of his voice. She summoned up an image of her parents who would be slyly watching the clock to see how long it took Trent and their daughter to get home. "My family. They saw us leave right behind them. If we're not home soon, they'll know—"

"They'll know what? That we stopped off along the way? Why should they be surprised? They realize we don't have much privacy at the lodge. They'll understand." His big hands were moving luxuriously over her, savoring the shape of her.

"Trent, I am not going to have everyone thinking that the first time I was alone with you I let you seduce me!"

"Why should you care what they think?" He was running his fingers around her waist now, moving lower until he found the curve of her buttocks. He cupped her and squeezed gently. "You're twenty-eight years old, and you've made certain everyone knows you're a big girl now. You can do what you want."

"Exactly," she managed, struggling for a measure of common sense. "And what I want is not to have everyone leering at me around the breakfast table tomorrow morning. I hardly know you, and I am not about to let you seduce me tonight in the front seat of a car."

"How about the back seat?" He nuzzled her ear beneath a fall of thick red hair. "God, you smell good."

"Trent, stop it." But she could already feel the change in him. There was a thread of good-humored resignation in his voice now. He wasn't going to push her any harder tonight.

"You're only postponing the inevitable, and I think you know it," he told her softly as he released her and assisted her back into her dress.

"No, I do not know that," she said tartly as she adjusted her clothing. "I don't know that at all. I didn't come home to have a summer fling with one of my parents' paying guests."

"Is there someone in Seattle?"

"There are lots of someones in Seattle."

"But no particular man?"

Filomena fastened her seat belt with a no-nonsense efficiency. "I don't think that's any business of yours. Take me home, Trent. It's getting late."

"If that's what you really want."

"It's what I want."

He turned the key in the ignition and drove silently back toward the main lake road. It wasn't until they were pulling into the lodge parking lot that he spoke.

"I was right," he said as if he were taking a great deal of satisfaction in something.

"Right about what?" Filomena gave him a suspicious glance.

"I could feel the passion in you just as easily as I can see ripples on a lake at dawn. It felt good, elf, even if it did leave me with an ache that's going to keep me awake half the night."

Filomena climbed out of the car and hurried toward the front door of her parents' home, which was just behind the main lodge.

As she fled up the steps she decided the evening hadn't turned out to be quite as amusing as she had anticipated, after all.

3

FILOMENA ENJOYED THE DRIVE from the lakeside lodge into the town of Gallant Lake the next morning. The day was fresh and clean and already turning very warm. The forest that edged the road sent wave after wave of glorious pine scent through the open window of the Porsche, and the car felt good, as it always did, under her hands.

Alone at last, she thought with a smile. True, she was on a mission for her mother, but that was all right. She didn't mind making herself useful by picking up more supplies for Shari's wedding. Besides, it was a great excuse to get away for a while.

She had faced the expected inquisition at breakfast, but she thought she had handled it well. Fortunately breakfast wasn't a very private affair when the family ate in the lodge dining room. Chatting with guests and making sure everyone was enjoying himself or herself was the primary goal at such times.

Amery and Trent had both been absent. They had left to go fishing before dawn and hadn't returned by seven-thirty. That had left Shari and Filomena's mother to conduct the investigation.

"Did you have a good time last night?" Shari had asked her older sister brightly as she'd poured herself a cup of coffee. Shari had her own cottage near the lake, but she frequently showed up for breakfast in the lodge dining room.

"I had a great time," Filomena had replied. When she hadn't volunteered anything further, her mother had entered the conversation.

"Isn't Trent Ravinder a nice man? We've so enjoyed having him at the lodge this summer. He's rapidly becoming one of the family. Your father says he's an excellent fishing partner. Amery finds him quite interesting."

"He's interesting, I'll grant you that," Filomena had responded. "But I'm not so sure I'd label him 'nice.'"

"Don't keep us in suspense. Get to the good stuff," Shari had said with a grin. "Did he finally make a pass on the way home last night? Mom says you were about twenty minutes later than she and Dad were getting home."

Filomena had smiled benignly. "I'm afraid Trent took a wrong turn. It delayed us somewhat."

Shari had doubled over with laughter. "Oh, no, I don't believe it."

"What? That he made a wrong turn? It's understandable. You know how many little side roads there are around these hills. Very easy to get off on the wrong track if you don't know where you're going."

"Hah. A wrong turn? When he had you along? Come off it, Fil. You were raised around here. You know all the back roads. He *did* make a pass, didn't he?" Shari's eyes had danced as she'd turned to her mother. "See? I told you. No need to fret about Fil making mischief with Brady Paxton. Trent's going to keep her out of trouble for us."

"Such a nice man," Meg Cromwell had repeated in heartfelt tones. "You know, Fil, lately I've been worrying that you might be getting a little too picky about your men these days. You're not getting any younger, you know, and the latest statistics claim it's getting harder and harder for women in your age group to find a husband."

Filomena had laughed. "For your information, Mom, I could get married any time I choose. You'd be amazed how many men become interested in matrimony when they find out how much money I'm making these days." Filomena's mouth had twisted wryly. "Believe me, the income from Cromwell & Sterling, Inc., is more than enough to compensate for all those dire statistics."

"Well, you wouldn't have to worry about Trent Ravinder marrying you just to get a share of Cromwell & Sterling," Meg had retorted. "The man gets paid a fortune by Asgard Development. In addition, he's done extremely well on his own in real estate. Your Uncle George says Trent has an instinct for land and how to make money with it. George should know. According to George, Trent could probably buy and sell Cromwell & Sterling if he wanted to do so."

"Somehow," Filomena had said thoughtfully, "that is not terribly reassuring."

"You're just being difficult," Shari had declared. "But be warned: Trent is closing in on you, and by the time you realize what's happening, it's going to be too late to run. Wait and see."

Filomena had sputtered slightly over her coffee, but the sputter had turned to laughter, and that had been the end of that topic of conversation.

Thinking about it now as she drove the curving road toward town, Filomena decided the morning inquisition could have been a lot worse. There was no doubt her parents and everyone else were quite taken with Trent Ravinder. Given the fact that they were also uneasy about any possible plans Filomena might have regarding Brady Paxton, it was understandable that they would all cheerfully conspire to push her and Trent together.

The only real mystery in the whole matter had been why Trent was allowing himself to be manipulated so easily. But perhaps that mystery had been cleared up last night when he had made that pass in the car.

He wanted her, and he was not averse to having her steered in his direction.

It made sense, Filomena thought, trying to be objective. Here he was spending several weeks in a relatively isolated location with only a small town nearby to provide entertainment. The possibility of a little dalliance with the innkeeper's daughter was probably not such an uninteresting proposition, especially since the innkeeper's daughter appeared old enough and savvy enough to know what she was doing. It was an added bonus that the innkeeper and his family were willing to aid and abet the affair.

There was only one drawback as far as Filomena could see and that was that, while she might be old enough to handle an affair with Trent Ravinder, she wasn't at all certain she was sufficiently savvy.

The truth was that Filomena's self-assurance had come from her business success and not from conducting a rousing love life. When one worked as hard as she had worked for the past nine years, there wasn't much time left over for an active love life, even if one had been interested in conducting affairs.

On top of that plain fact, there had been an added complication for Filomena. She knew deep inside she wasn't really cut out for a series of light and scintillating affairs. Perhaps she was too much of a small-town girl at heart, or perhaps she knew she was inclined to care too much when she allowed herself to care at all. Whatever the reason, she wasn't interested in a summer fling with Trent Ravinder or anyone else.

But as she pondered the matter of dealing with Trent, Filomena admitted to herself it wasn't going to be simple to keep him at a distance. That kiss in the front seat of the Mercedes had told her that much. It had forced her to confront the fact that she was attracted to the man, and she knew now he definitely wanted her. They were going to be spending the next few weeks in close proximity. That was a dangerous mixture. As far as she was concerned it was much more dangerous than anything that could possibly happen with Brady Paxton. She wondered why her family didn't see that as clearly as she did.

Probably because they seemed to have a sort of blind faith and trust in Trent. She could not really blame them. Ravinder had a way of commanding respect and trust.

Filomena parked the Porsche in front of the bank with a flourish. She knew she had an audience, and she didn't want to disappoint them. Bounding out of the car, she waved cheerfully at several people who recognized her and the vehicle. She grinned to herself when she saw them stare appreciatively at the Porsche and then at the slick little white summer dress with the wide, gutsy belt she was wearing. She knew the outfit fitted perfectly and that it had a definite rakish charm.

The mission for her mother was soon accomplished, but when she had stashed the supplies in the back of the Porsche, Filomena decided she wasn't ready to head back to the lodge immediately. Trent would be there by now, and she still hadn't made up her mind about how to handle him.

A cup of coffee in the small restaurant next to the bank was an appealing option. She walked through the door and was immediately hailed by the middle-aged woman behind the counter.

"Well, as I live and breathe, it really is you, isn't it, Fil? Someone told me that was your hot little car out front, and I couldn't believe it. Haven't seen you in a month of Sundays. Let's have a look at you, girl. That is some outfit you've got on. Turn around and let's see the back."

Filomena obediently twirled around and showed off the triangle cutout that revealed a tantalizing glimpse of skin and the black buttons that marked the open slit at the hemline of the skirt. "Well? What do you think, Muriel? We're putting this into our resort collection this winter."

"You want my opinion?" Muriel chuckled with disbelief. "It's as cute as a bug's ear, but I'm no fashion expert, and you know it. Sure looks good on you, though. You've changed some, haven't you? Heard you wowed a few people at the country club last night."

Filomena winced. "You mean you've already had a report on what happened at the club last night?"

"You know how fast gossip travels around here. I also heard about that nice talk you gave to the local girls' club a few days ago. You really dazzled 'em."

"Girls that age are always fascinated with fashion and style." Filomena smiled slightly, remembering the amused tolerance in Trent's eyes when word had gotten back to the lodge about Filomena's highly successful talk. He hadn't said a word, but she had known exactly what he was thinking. *Another show for the hometown crowd.*

Muriel chuckled. "From what I hear, it wasn't just the talk on fashion you gave that interested them. You made a big point of letting them know that, if they were willing to work, they could grow up to be as successful as you've been. Good for young girls to hear that. I could have used a few lectures like that when I was growing up. Young girls need to know there's something out there besides boys."

"I gave them my opinion on boys while I was giving them the lecture on success," Filomena said.

"I heard." Muriel winked. "Something about treating boys like candy, wasn't it? Too much will rot your teeth."

"I hope they got the point," Filomena said with an answering smile.

"Even if they didn't, the volunteers who run that club sure appreciated the donation you made. Heaven knows they can use the money. They do a good job with those kids. Sit down and tell me what you've been doing with yourself."

Muriel reached for the coffeepot and took a seat in the booth across from Filomena. They chatted for fifteen or twenty minutes until the small café began to fill up with a late-morning coffee crowd. Muriel finally excused herself reluctantly.

"Sorry, but it looks like I'm going to have to get to work. You sit still and finish your coffee, Fil. I hear you're going to be around a while this summer, so maybe we'll get another chance to chat, hmm?"

"Don't worry, I plan to be here a while. I'll stop in again."

"You do that. Say hello to your mother for me."

"I will, Muriel."

Muriel went back around behind the counter, and Filomena picked up her coffee mug. She was sipping slowly, gazing pensively out the window at a street of shops that had changed very little since she had left town, when she sensed someone near her shoulder. Filomena stifled a groan and looked up.

"Hello, Brady."

"Hi, Fil. Someone said that was your green Porsche outside, so I decided to see if you were in here having a cup of coffee. I could use one myself." He sat down without waiting for an invitation and signaled Muriel for coffee. "That's quite a car, Fil. A real honey." He leaned forward, folded his arms on the counter and smiled.

Filomena remembered that smile. It had once seemed boyish and intimate and sexy. Now, after nine years in the hard world of business, she recognized the expression for what it was, a salesman's smile. Her mouth tilted in private amusement as she thought about just how naive she had been when she was nineteen. "I'm rather fond of that car myself."

"Did you have a good time last night, Fil?" Brady asked as Muriel poured the coffee.

Filomena caught the faint disapproval in Muriel's gaze before the older woman bustled back to the counter. "Terrific. What about you?"

Brady shrugged. "The usual. Gloria and I have been going out to the country club almost every Saturday night for nine years. Talk about being in a rut."

Filomena wondered where the conversation was going. "It's a nice place," she commented neutrally.

"It must seem pretty tame to you after all the world travel and city living you've been doing for the past few years." Brady's gaze became intent and curious. "You've really changed, haven't you, Fil? That car, those clothes and—" he made an all-encompassing movement with one hand "—and everything."

Filomena knew the "and everything" was Brady's attempt to describe the self-confidence she hadn't had at nineteen. She smiled slightly. "Time doesn't stand still, Brady. I've been busy during the past few years."

"So I've heard." He leaned forward even more, striving for an air of greater intimacy. "Do you ever think about the old days, Fil? About us?"

"Nope," she said cheerfully.

"I do," he said bluntly.

"Waste of time, Brady."

"But you must wonder sometimes what we missed together, you and me," he murmured.

"I don't have much time for that kind of wondering. I've got too much going on in my life."

"I think about it a lot." He looked down at his coffee and then raised his eyes. "Gloria and me, well, it didn't quite turn out the way I thought it would."

"Things rarely do turn out the way we think they will. But in my case, they definitely turned out better than anything I could have imagined when I was nineteen. Sorry about your situation, but that's the way it goes, I guess."

"You've never married," Brady pointed out, as if the fact was evidence of her lingering heartache.

"Haven't had time for that, either."

"I burned you pretty bad, huh?"

Filomena grinned. "You want the truth, Brady? Finding you and Gloria in bed together that day was the best thing that ever happened to me. I've been profoundly grateful to both of you ever since. When I think of what I would have missed if I'd married you . . ." She let the sentence trail off and shook her head. "I get cold chills down my spine. Believe me, Brady, I can't thank you enough for ending our engagement."

A flash of anger appeared in Brady's eyes, and his mouth tightened briefly. Then he said coldly, "I suppose you've been through a lot of men in the past few years.

Is this Ravinder guy going to be another scalp on your belt?"

Filomena felt her temper start to rise, and then she was laughing softly instead. "That's an interesting image." She wondered what Ravinder would say to becoming a scalp on her belt. The truth was, she was far more likely to become one on his if she wasn't careful.

"What's so funny?" Brady's voice turned belligerent.

"Never mind." She finished her coffee and reached for her purse. "Well, Brady, I hate to rush off, but Mom's waiting for me. I'd better be on my way."

"Fil, wait." He put out a placating hand. "I want to talk to you."

"I don't think we have much to say to each other, Brady."

"Damn it, this is important, Fil. It's business."

She eyed him warily. "What kind of business?"

"Real estate business." Brady hunched closer yet and lowered his voice. "Fil, I know Ravinder's in town to check out lakefront property for Asgard."

"He says he's not."

"What do you expect him to do? Blurt it out? Take my word for it, he's here on business. You know, you can do me and some other folks a big favor, Fil."

"I doubt it," she retorted lightly, knowing now exactly where the conversation was going.

"There's a cut in it for you," Brady said slyly. "I hear you're a hotshot business lady these days. Well, this should definitely interest you. Growing businesses always need capital. Don't try to tell me your company couldn't use some."

Filomena didn't bother. The truth was, Brady was right. Cromwell & Sterling was actively searching for capital at that very moment. She decided it was probably better if Brady didn't know that, however, so she kept her mouth shut.

"There's money in this, Fil. I guarantee it. All you have to do is use your influence on Ravinder to find out exactly what area of the lake he's interested in picking up for Asgard. I've got options on a lot of property around here. I've formed a real estate partnership operation that's been picking land up over the years just on the chance that something like this would happen. Find out which way Ravinder's going to move, and I can exercise my options on the right parcel. Then we can turn around and sell the land to Asgard."

"At about triple the value?" Filomena asked politely.

"That's what business is all about, Fil." Brady gave her an impatient look. "This could be our big chance. There's a fortune in this if we play our cards right."

"And I'm the card you want to play, is that it?"

"Look, you've got the inside track. Ravinder's interested in you. Any fool can see that. All you have to do is play up to him, get him to talk, feel him out. Finding out what he's going to recommend to Asgard should be easy for you. My partners and I would pay you a commission if the deal goes through, say five percent."

"Your generosity overwhelms me." Filomena made another move to get out of the booth.

"All right, eight percent. Fil, what's the big problem? You're probably sleeping with him already, right?"

"Wrong." Filomena realized with a sense of amazement that she was suddenly on the verge of losing her temper, really losing it. It took a lot these days, but it could still happen. Her eyes chilled as she met Brady's gaze across the table. "I am not sleeping with him, and for your information, I resent the implication that I am. I am a businesswoman, not a prostitute, and if you imply otherwise once more I will announce to the entire town exactly what you're asking me to do. I will also tell Trent Ravinder, which should put paid to your ideas of making a killing on your land options. Do we understand each other, Brady?"

"Calm down, Fil. What the hell's the matter with you? If you're a businesswoman, then you know damn well I'm only talking common sense. You're in a position to help an old friend and make a nice little commission yourself on the side. It's not like I'm asking you to seduce the guy. It's obvious you two already have something going. Think about it, Fil, that's all I'm saying. Just think about it."

Filomena smiled dangerously. "Brady, *old friend*, I learned everything I needed to know about you nine years ago, and the most important thing I learned was that you can't be trusted. I never get involved in business arrangements with people I can't trust. I'm sure you can understand that. It's just common sense. Goodbye, Brady. Go home to your wife. You wanted her badly enough nine years ago." She started to slide out of the booth.

Brady looked at her knowingly. "You still haven't gotten over it, have you, Fil? You're still hurting because of what happened back then. That's why you've never married, isn't it? That's why you're so upset. But things are different now. I've changed and you've changed. You're a much more interesting woman these days. This time around we could really have something together, you and I."

"Don't hold your breath, Brady," Filomena said bluntly, and turned to walk out of the restaurant. She was aware of the interested glances from Muriel and the other customers, but she was too angry to pay much attention. Brady Paxton hadn't changed much over the years. He was still a snake. She felt sorry for Gloria, who by now had probably discovered that for herself.

Filomena tossed her purse onto the passenger seat of the Porsche and slipped behind the wheel. As soon as she felt the familiar confines of the car, she began to relax. She shouldn't have let Brady get to her. She wouldn't have if he hadn't thrown her relationship with Trent Ravinder in her face and asked her to spy on the man.

Being asked to betray Ravinder really did something to her normally placid temper. She shuddered to think what Trent himself would have to say if he knew what had just happened.

Better to let sleeping dogs lie, Filomena thought as she put the Porsche in gear and pulled out onto the main road. Trent claimed he was here for a vacation, and she was inclined to believe him. Whatever else you could say about the man, he appeared to be rigid on the subject of honesty and his own integrity. He wouldn't lie, and he wouldn't take kindly to the idea that someone was plotting to use Filomena against him. No sense risking his temper. It was probably a heck of a lot worse than her own.

By the time she was pulling into the parking lot of the Gallant Lake Lodge, Filomena's mood was back to normal. She got out of the car and began retrieving the packages she had stashed in the back.

"I'll give you a hand," Trent said behind her.

Filomena straightened abruptly, startled by the sound of his voice. She blinked as she looked at him in the sunlight. He seemed very large standing there in his faded denims, plaid shirt and scuffed boots. Very large and very much at home in the setting of lake and trees and sky. He didn't look at all like a high-powered businessman today. He looked more like a man who made his living working outdoors with his hands.

"Hi, Trent," Filomena said politely, automatically edging a couple of steps away from him. It was a habit she had around large males. "How was the fishing?"

"The fishing was fine. It usually is with your father along." He took one of the packages out of her arms and eyed her assessingly. "Why do you do that?"

"Do what?"

"Move away from me whenever I get close."

Filomena shrugged as she started up the path toward her parents' quarters. "I just don't like people looming over me, that's all."

"Especially men?" he asked politely as he followed her up the path.

"Especially men," she agreed sweetly. "They tend to block the light. Are we eating the fish you caught for lunch today?"

"I don't know what the others are eating, but you and I are going to have tuna fish sandwiches, dill pickles and chips."

She stopped and swung around in surprise. "We are?"

"Uh-huh." Trent looked pleased with himself. "You and I are going on a picnic. Your mother had the chef pack us a lunch. How long has it been since you've been on a picnic, Filomena?"

"Ages," she admitted, continuing to stare at him uncertainly. A picnic meant being alone with Trent. She wasn't sure that was such a good idea.

"Relax," he said softly, as if he'd read her mind. "I'll try not to block out too much of the light."

Filomena found herself responding to the invitation and the reassurance in his eyes. There was no need to let him know she was wary of him. It was embarrassing and annoying. After all, she wasn't a nervous, unsophisticated teenager. "Well," she said thoughtfully, "it is a lovely day for a picnic, isn't it?"

His grin was slow and compelling. "Yes," he said. "It is."

FORTY MINUTES LATER Trent finally pronounced himself satisfied with the picnic location Filomena had suggested. She'd chosen a pebbly beach near the lake. There were several convenient boulders to provide seating, and in the trees behind them was a cool, shaded forest floor covered with pine needles. Best of all there was plenty of privacy. Trent speculated on how difficult it might be to get Filomena down onto that bed of pine.

It would probably be extremely difficult initially, but once he had her down there he was fairly certain he could convince her to stay. He knew now he could make her want him. Probably not as much as he wanted her, but he was willing to work on that part. It was just a matter of time, and he had the next few weeks ahead of him.

He watched as she unpacked the picnic basket. Her red hair shone in the sunlight that filtered through the trees. She had changed into a pair of jeans and a teal-blue shirt that was cut in a man's style yet somehow seemed to emphasize her femininity.

Trent tormented himself with visions of shaping Filomena's nicely rounded buttocks in his hands and lifting her up against his chest so that he could feel her soft, pert breasts. The images burned in his mind until he felt the sudden tightness of the denim below his waist. His body was already reacting strongly to the fantasy.

Trent stifled a rueful curse and unobtrusively shifted his position slightly as he lounged back against a boulder. Filomena's effect on him could be embarrassing at times.

He didn't know whether to be relieved or annoyed that she seemed totally unaware of it.

"How was the drive into town?" Trent made himself ask conversationally. He had already decided to keep this picnic scene as casual and unthreatening as possible. Last night he had confirmed the physical attraction between them. For a few minutes there in the front seat of the Mercedes, she had practically melted in his arms. Now that he knew for certain that she would respond to him when the time came, he could afford to take it easy.

"Fine. I was just on an errand for my mother."

"Your dad says you drive that Porsche as if you were practicing for the Indianapolis 500. I'm inclined to agree with him."

Filomena chuckled. "Does that bother you, too? Poor Trent. You've taken on a terrible responsibility if you're going to start worrying about everything from my clothes to my driving. You'll be gray in no time."

"I can see why Amery worries about you."

Filomena took a sizable chunk out of her sandwich and chewed enthusiastically. "My parents have always worried about me. They used to worry because I didn't have a social life in high school. Shari, who's nearly two years younger than me, had all the dates she wanted from the moment my father allowed her out of the house at night. I always sat home and read or baby-sat. Shari was on the cheerleading squad. I never even went to the games. Then I started seeing Brady during my first year of college, and they really panicked."

"They didn't like him?"

"They thought he was taking advantage of me, just toying with me," Filomena said smoothly. "They weren't alone. Everyone wondered what Brady saw in me. That did a lot for my ego, as you can imagine. When it turned out everyone was right about Brady, my family worried about me again. They knew how humiliated I'd been. When I went back to college in the fall, they were all relieved for a while until I entered a fine arts program instead of taking more useful classes. When Glenna and I opened our own business three years ago, Mom and Dad panicked again. They just knew it would fail because I didn't have the vaguest notion of how to run a business. But they forgot that I'm a fast learner." Filomena laughed at him with her eyes. "Shall I go on?"

"I think I get the picture. So now you're back in town and the family has something new to worry about."

"Lots of new things to worry about apparently. It isn't just this business about whether or not I'm going to cause a scandal with Brady. Now Mom has started to get nervous about the fact that I'm twenty-eight years old and not married. She's been reading too many statistics, it seems. When I tell her I'm not particularly interested in marriage, she really frets."

"Is that true? You're really not interested in marriage?" That bothered him. She was an independent little thing. He was glad she hadn't married Paxton when she was nineteen, but it annoyed him to think she might still be off marriage.

"Frankly, I've got other, more important things going on in my life at the moment."

"Such as?"

"It's a business matter." She looked at him. "Do you really want to hear about it?"

"Sure." He told himself he needed to know as much about her as possible. "I'm a businessman myself, remember?"

"When I see you dressed like that, it's easy to forget."

"It's a mistake to let one segment of your life dominate all the others," Trent said seriously. "I've been learning that lesson lately."

"Is that why you're taking a long vacation this summer? Trying to get some balance in your life?"

Her unexpected insight astonished him. His eyes met hers. "How did you guess?"

"I don't know," she confessed. "But most high-powered business people don't take six weeks off at a time. The pressure is too great. If, as you claim, you're not here to scout for Asgard, then you really must be on an extended vacation. It just struck me that maybe you're here to, well, look for something. Something personal."

"You are a shrewd woman, Filomena. You're right. I am here to look for something. I'm thirty-six years old, and there are some things missing in my life. I came here to sort through my priorities and decide what I really want."

Her eyes were warm with understanding. "You're a smart man and a brave one. Not everyone has the courage to assess his life and make major decisions about it. Most people find it easier to drift."

"I think I'm in the middle of a mid-life crisis."

She shook her head. "No, it's not a crisis. Not when you control the situation and handle it rationally the way you're doing."

Trent began to feel uneasy. He had brought her here to learn more about her. Instead she was the one conducting the psychological probe. It was time to get things back on track. "Tell me about the business matter that's more important to you than marriage."

She laughed. "Just a normal business decision. My partner and I have decided to expand. We're thinking about opening our own shops instead of selling just through the major department store chains. It would allow us a lot more flexibility." Her voice reflected her enthusiasm for the project as she spoke. "We're also considering adding a line of sports clothes for larger women, the ones who are on the other side of the average scale. They've been as overlooked by the designers as we shorter types have been."

Trent nodded, the business side of his nature momentarily coming to the fore. "Where are you going to get the capital for that kind of expansion?"

"That's part of the problem," she admitted. "But Glenna and I are working on it. We've got a loan application into a bank that financed us three years ago. They were reasonably supportive in the past, and I think they will be again."

"Maybe you shouldn't try to do both projects at once," Trent suggested. "Opening your own shops is going to be a very expensive proposition, and so is starting a new line of clothing. Pick the one you think you can handle and let the other idea ride for a while."

She flashed him a piercing look. "You're hardly an expert on the fashion business."

"True, but I am an expert on such basics as the dangers of overexpansion and the problems of finding financial resources. Maybe you and your partner should get a financial consultant in to look over your situation before you go off in a direction that could sink you and your firm. I know a good man in Seattle named Handel. He's made a specialty out of advising growing businesses like yours. He knows how critical these expansion stages are. A lot of companies collapse at this point in their development."

"If I want your advice," she said dryly, "I'll ask for it."

"I doubt it. You've probably decided I'm not qualified to advise you on the grounds that I'm too large."

She stared at him for a second and then burst into laughter.

Trent began to relax. It was going to be all right, he told himself. He could handle her. She was a challenge, but he was good at responding to challenges. All he needed was time.

Time and opportunity.

He would have time this summer, but he began to worry about opportunity. It wasn't going to be easy enticing Filomena Cromwell into a love affair when her whole family and a good portion of the local residents would be watching with avid interest. Filomena herself was too busy putting on her flashy show for the hometown folks. She was having too much fun being a big fish in a small pond. It wasn't going to be simple to distract her long enough to lure her into his arms.

He watched her eat a dill pickle and told himself that somehow, some way, he had to get her into bed. He had to find a way to overcome her wariness, a way past that slick, polished facade. Above all, he wanted to teach her that she could trust him. But he was going to have to get her full attention first.

Based on what he had learned last night when he'd held her in his arms, he had a hunch the fastest way to accomplish his goal was to awaken the passion she kept leashed inside her.

Opportunity, he told himself again. That was what he needed. He had been in the business world long enough to know that sometimes a man had to create his own opportunities. He let the conversation wander off into a variety of pleasant byways while he considered his problem.

Two hours after they had left the lodge, Trent and Filomena returned. They walked across the wide lawn toward the terrace of her parents' home, where Amery, Meg and Shari were sitting with glasses of iced tea. Trent had just decided that the afternoon had been a reasonable success and was congratulating himself on his clever handling of Filomena when the tension of the three people seated around the table finally got through to him.

It seemed to get through to Filomena at the same time.

"Hey, what's up? You three look as if you just got advance word of an earthquake," she remarked cheerfully.

Amery glanced at Trent and then at his daughter. "I don't think it's quite that serious. But you managed to shake Meg and Shari up a bit along with a fair number of neighbors."

Filomena's eyebrows rose. "Is that right? How did I do that?"

Meg Cromwell sighed. "I know there's nothing to the tale, dear, but you know how rumors fly around here. We heard you met Brady Paxton in town this morning. Someone said you'd been seen sharing coffee with him at Muriel's café. And if we've heard it, you can bet everyone else in Gallant Lake has, too, including Gloria."

Trent felt all his good resolutions about taking his time with Filomena go up in a cloud of smoke. This, he decided, was what came of giving a woman too much time, especially a woman who was endowed with a bent toward mischief and who had an old score to settle.

"Apparently I'm not doing my job properly," he remarked coolly.

Filomena whirled on him. "What's that supposed to mean?" she demanded in ominous tones.

"IT LOOKS LIKE I'll have to pay more attention to the task of keeping an eye on you," Trent said a little too casually.

Filomena stiffened at the implied accusation. She saw the anxiety in her mother's eyes and was furious with whoever had relayed the story of her unwelcome chat with Brady Paxton. Shari and her father didn't appear as upset as her mother, but there was no doubt that the news had made them uneasy. Most of all, Filomena was aware of the cool, possessive watchfulness in Trent.

"You've assured me you're not here to work this summer, Trent, so don't start worrying about the job of keeping me out of trouble," she said icily.

"Hey," Shari put in quickly, "he was just teasing you, Fil."

"No, I wasn't," Trent said calmly. He reached for the pitcher of iced tea and poured himself a glass. "I was dead serious. No more unsupervised trips into town for you, Filomena. You're obviously incapable of steering clear of trouble. You can't resist putting on your show for the locals, can you? Fortunately for you I'm willing to keep an eye on you."

"Oh, gee, thanks." A flash of recklessness went through her. She put her hands on her hips and regarded Trent and her family with narrowed eyes. "Would you all like to know exactly what happened this morning at Muriel's? I'll tell you. I was sitting there alone, enjoying a quiet cup of coffee, when Brady came in and sat down across from me. Guess what he wanted."

"Uh, I think we can all guess what he wanted," Amery said uncomfortably.

"Sure," said Shari. "Everyone knows he'd jump at the chance to have a fling with you this summer. He's restless and bored and everybody in town knows it."

"Is that right? Well, I've got news for you. What he wanted was for me to pump Trent for information on Asgard Development's plans for a resort here on the lake. He's convinced Trent's here to scout the territory for Asgard. Furthermore, Brady offered me a nice little commission if I'd get the information for him and his real estate partnership cronies. There. Does that answer all your questions?" Filomena lifted her chin in triumphant challenge.

"Oh, dear," Meg said. "How awkward."

Shari was grinning. "Trust old Brady to put business before pleasure."

Amery groaned. "I should have known. I've heard Paxton's got options on some prime land around the lake."

It was Trent who put the next question to Filomena. He grinned at her over the rim of his tea glass. "You haven't told us yet whether or not you're going to do it."

"Do what?" Filomena demanded.

"Pump me for the information about Asgard's development plans."

"You don't look particularly worried," she muttered. The rush of recklessness faded as she realized Trent wasn't going to rise to the bait.

"Probably because I've already told you Asgard doesn't have any plans for Gallant Lake, and I think you believe me. But I won't mind if you try to worm the details of our lack of plans out of me."

He looked so expectant that Filomena felt her annoyance begin to melt. Her sense of humor resurfaced. "Too late. I already told Brady you didn't have any plans, and he didn't give me a dime for the information."

"Probably because he didn't believe you," Trent said.

"Probably," she agreed, remembering the depth of Brady's conviction on the subject. She smiled faintly. "That's his problem."

"Yes," he agreed blandly, "it is."

Shari spoke up. "That reminds me," she said quickly, "you may have some problems of your own, Trent. There was a call for you from Portland an hour ago. You're to contact a Mr. Reece as soon as possible."

Trent's good humor vanished. "Reece called?"

Shari nodded. "The front desk took the call and gave the message to me. They figured one of the family would see you first. Bad news?"

"No, not really." Trent finished his iced tea. "Reece is my assistant. He had instructions not to bother me here unless it was important. I guess something's come up. Excuse me while I return that call."

Amery got to his feet. "I'd better get back to the office. I've still got a lot of work ahead of me this afternoon."

Meg nodded and put down her half-finished iced tea. "And I've got to have a chat with the chef. I'll see you all at dinner."

"I'll come with you, Mom," Shari said. "I want to talk to Henry about my wedding cake. He's got to understand that I want a decent tasting frosting, not one that's just designed to hold pretty shapes."

When Filomena looked around a moment later, she had the patio to herself. With a relieved sigh, she flopped down in one of the lounge chairs and poured herself the last of the iced tea. Life could be stressful at times.

IT WASN'T UNTIL he finished the terse call with Hal Reece that Trent finally realized the potential of the opportunity that had just been dangled in front of him.

He was a man who knew how to grab opportunities when they appeared. He couldn't afford to ignore this one, especially now that Filomena was showing signs of needing a firmer hand.

He sat on the edge of his bed, elbows resting on his thighs, his big hands clasped loosely between his knees as he stared thoughtfully into space. Mentally he looked at this golden opportunity from every angle, searching for flaws, dangers and possible explosive points. It was risky, but it just might work. If it did work, he would have solved the problem of finding both time and opportunity to forge a way through Filomena's slick facade.

He sat very quietly for another ten minutes, planning for as many unknowns as he could. Then he got to his feet and went in search of Filomena.

FILOMENA WAS STILL ENJOYING her solitude on the patio after everyone else's departure when she heard her parents' private phone ring through the open sliding glass doors behind her.

Reluctantly she put down the copy of *Vogue* she had been scanning and went inside to answer the summons. It would probably be a friend of her mother's, inquiring about shower-gift ideas for Shari. That was all right, Filomena thought. She was equipped to answer any question in that line. She had lots of gift ideas in mind for Shari.

"Cromwell residence," she said cheerfully as she snatched the receiver out of its cradle.

"You think you're so damn smart, don't you?" a woman's voice snapped. Whoever it was sounded wretched with fury. There was a choking sob before she continued. "You think you can just come back after all this time and take him away from me, but you're wrong. You're nothing but a little tramp, and I'm going to make sure everyone knows it. You think it's a lot of fun to make a spectacle of yourself? Are you getting a kick out of racing around in that expensive car and showing off your fancy clothes while you dangle yourself in front of every man in town?"

"Gloria?" Filomena was stunned by the venom in the woman's voice. "Hold on a second. You've got no reason to yell at me. Just calm down—"

"Calm down!" Gloria's voice rose to an agonized shriek. "Calm down while you seduce my husband? Calm down while you wiggle your tail in front of him every time you get near him? You were a silly, unsophisticated, ugly little fool nine years ago, Filomena Cromwell. But you haven't changed for the better. You've just succeeded in turning yourself into a rich, flashy little bitch. But I won't let you get your hands on my husband. Do you hear me? I know you're after revenge, but you're not going to get it!"

"Believe me, Gloria, I don't have any desire to get my hands on Brady. He's all yours, and you're welcome to him." Filomena tried to keep her tones soothing, but she had a sick feeling she was only stoking the fires of resentment and anger that were burning in Gloria Paxton.

"Don't lie to me," Gloria raged. "I saw you looking at him last night. You want to prove you can get him back, don't you? It's not as though you still love him. You just want to prove something!"

Filomena held the phone away from her ear. Gloria's words were coming through so loudly that they were audible at some distance. "Gloria, listen to me, you've got it all wrong."

"No, you listen to me, you little tramp. I heard you met Brady in town this morning. I know all about your private meeting at Muriel's."

"Private! Everyone in town has coffee there."

"And you knew I'd find out, didn't you? You're trying to punish me as well as seduce my husband. But it won't work. I won't let you. He didn't want you when you were nineteen, you fool. He was just bored that year, and you were available. He was just playing with you. He told me so. He used to laugh about what a little twit you were, and I used to laugh with him. Do you hear me?"

Before Filomena could respond, the phone on the other end was slammed down with such force that she flinched. She stood very still for several seconds, listening to the loud dial tone.

"What's the matter, Filomena?" Trent asked quietly behind her. "Finding out there are a few perils and pitfalls in this game of coming back to the old hometown and showing everyone how you've changed?"

Filomena jumped, whirling around in surprise. For an instant she knew the chagrin she was feeling was visible in her eyes. She realized it because of the way Trent was studying her so intently. He leaned against the jamb in the open doorway, his arms folded across his broad chest. He was a perceptive man, she thought distractedly. Too perceptive by far.

"I'm not playing games, Trent. I'm simply here to enjoy a few weeks of vacation. But I seem to be having a hard time convincing anyone of that fact."

"Especially Gloria Paxton, I'll bet. That was her on the phone just now, I take it? Warning you off her husband?"

Slowly Filomena replaced the instrument. "I told her there was no need."

"Uh-huh. Do you honestly expect her to believe you? She's scared of being put through the same kind of humiliation she and Brady put you through nine years ago. As far as she's concerned, you're the enemy. People don't always react rationally when they're frightened. Especially if they've got good reason to be nervous in the first place."

"She's got no reason to worry about me running off with Brady!" Filomena snapped. She swung around and stalked to the huge picture window that overlooked the lake.

"She thinks she has. And so does just about everyone else in town apparently."

"Well, they can just chew their fingernails down to the quick worrying about it as far as I'm concerned."

"The people who are watching you this time are the same ones who watched you when you were nineteen, aren't they? It must be satisfying to show them you're not the one to be pitied this time around."

"I am *not* here to prove I can take Brady Paxton back. I don't want him. I'll admit it's fun to let everyone know I've made a success of myself, but that's all I'm interested in doing," Filomena said in a grim whisper. "No one seems willing to believe that."

"I believe it," Trent said coolly.

Filomena experienced a rush of relief that was almost startling. Someone believed her. She clamped down on the sensation and nodded politely. "Thank you."

"You're welcome," he said dryly. "I know what it's like not to have anyone believe you. It gets to the point where you feel like you're beating your head against a stone wall."

His words surprised her. Filomena glanced at him over her shoulder. "Is that right?"

He didn't move, just stood there watching her with that curious intensity. "Yes. But my understanding isn't going to do much good. You're a walking keg of dynamite as far as everyone else is concerned."

Filomena made a face. "Not a pleasant thought, is it?"

"If you're interested, I have a suggestion to make, one that might relieve some of the tension that seems to be building up around you."

She glanced at him quickly. "What kind of suggestion?"

"A practical one. It would give everyone something else to talk about besides you and Paxton."

"And how am I supposed to do that?"

"I have to drive to Portland this afternoon. Business. I'll be staying the night and returning in the morning. Come with me, Filomena."

Filomena caught her breath, unable to look away from his jade gaze. "With you?" she echoed faintly.

"You can spend the night with Reece and his wife. We'll have dinner with them and then you can go back to their place, if that's what you want."

"I don't like to impose on strangers." Her voice sounded weak and breathless, even to her own ears.

"Then you can stay in a hotel, or . . ." He let the sentence trail off.

"Or what?"

"Or you can stay with me at my apartment," he finished bluntly. "The choice will be yours, I promise."

Filomena couldn't seem to organize the chaotic thoughts that were suddenly filling her brain. She could hear Gloria Paxton's voice screaming in her ears, could still see the concern and anxiety in her mother's eyes. Filomena thought of the shower she was supposed to attend tonight, and the realization that every other guest would be speculating about her and Brady was more than she wanted to face. It might be nice to get away for a while.

Going to Portland with Trent suddenly looked like a reasonable escape. She made up her mind with the quick, firm resolve she was accustomed to exercising in business. "All right, Trent. Thank you for the invitation. Maybe a day or two away from here is just what the situation calls for. I'll go pack."

"It's nearly a three-hour drive," Trent said. "I want to leave as soon as possible."

Filomena nodded and turned to go to her room. "I won't keep you waiting."

THE DRIVE TO PORTLAND turned out to be a surprisingly pleasant experience. The farther she got from Gallant Lake, the more Filomena began to relax. It made her realize just how tense she had been after Gloria's phone call.

Her family had been temporarily astonished when she had informed them of her decision, but there had been no doubt about the relief that had followed. No one had asked where she would be staying, and that had annoyed Filomena for some reason. Her family didn't seem to have any objections to the possibility of her running off to Portland for a one-night stand with Trent Ravinder if it meant she wouldn't be around to cause any trouble with the Paxtons back in Gallant Lake. That rankled.

"What's the matter?" Trent asked casually at one point during the trip.

"I was just thinking that no one asked where I would be staying tonight. All that fuss about having a little cup of coffee with Brady, yet no one says a word about me dashing off to Portland with you for a whole night."

Trent slid her a quick, assessing glance. "You're an adult. As long as you aren't causing anyone any trouble, your family is content to let you make your own decisions."

"It doesn't strike you as slightly hypocritical?"

"No. You going with me to Portland is an entirely different situation than you driving Gloria Paxton crazy with jealousy."

"Oh, I see," Filomena said too brightly. "Well, that explains it, of course. No one minds if I sleep with you, so long as I don't show any signs of wanting to seduce Brady. Is that it?"

"That's it," he said in a mock-congratulatory tone. "No wonder you've done so well in the business world, Filomena. You're very good at putting two and two together."

A slow, unwilling smile tugged at her mouth. "It's a wonder you've survived at all. I would have thought by now that someone might have clobbered you on general principles."

"It's been tried a time or two." He shrugged. "But when it comes to defending principles, I always win."

"Because you don't give an inch?"

"Right."

"Just what is this all-important business that's forcing you to return to Portland on the spur of the moment?"

He gave her a sharp glance. "The business is for real," he said crisply. "I didn't invent it as an excuse to lure you to Portland."

She heard the familiar arrogance in his voice and put up a hand. "Okay, I believe you. What is it?"

He seemed to relax slightly. "Asgard's been trying to close a deal for some property over on the coast for three months. The old man who owns the land has been unwilling to sell because he was afraid of what would happen to the place afterward. He needs the money, but he doesn't want to see his family land covered with a bunch of ugly condos and shopping centers. I've shown him the plans Asgard has for the place and assured him that the architect's rendering is accurate and will be adhered to. Asgard wants to put in a quiet luxury resort and will spend a lot of money making sure the land retains its original appeal. It won't be ruined with parking lots and shopping malls. Apparently the owner is finally ready to sign."

"And you have to be there when he does?"

"The old man doesn't trust development companies," Trent explained wryly.

"But he trusts you?"

"Yes."

They reached Portland shortly before five, and Trent drove immediately to the downtown offices of Asgard Development. A harried-looking man in his early thirties with thinning hair and a quick smile was waiting for Trent in an eighth-floor office that had a view of the Willamette River. He got to his feet as Trent walked through the door.

"About time you got here, Trent. Baldwin has been sticking to his guns, just as I told you on the phone. Won't sign a damn thing until you shake hands with him on the deal and assure him everything's going to be just as stipulated in the plans." The man broke off as he caught sight of Filomena. "Excuse me, ma'am. I didn't see you. Please come in."

"Filomena, this is Hal Reece. Reece, this is Filomena Cromwell, a friend of mine." Trent made the introductions quickly, his attention obviously on the business at hand.

"Pleased to meet you, Filomena. Trent said he might be bringing someone with him. You'll join us for dinner?"

"Thank you," Filomena murmured.

"Where's Baldwin and the paperwork?" Trent interrupted to ask.

"I've got him waiting down the hall in a conference room. Asgard is there, too, but Baldwin won't take his word for anything. The guy is only willing to trust you."

"Doesn't he realize he's got a solid legal contract that stipulates how the land can be developed?"

"Asgard has explained it to him several times. But Baldwin wants to see you before he signs. He's got a point, Trent. Once that land officially belongs to Asgard, we can do anything we want with it. Baldwin knows that and doesn't want to take any chances. You ready?"

"Sure." Trent turned to Filomena. "You can wait in the outer office, if you like. We'll be through in a half hour or so. Then we'll go have a drink and some dinner with Reece and his wife."

Filomena nodded, glancing around the office in open curiosity. "Don't worry about me. I'll be fine."

Reece saw her appraising glance and chuckled. "Trent's offices are upstairs, if you're interested. His secretary's gone home for the day, but you're welcome to snoop around, if you like. He's got a much wider view of the river than I do."

Filomena smiled. "Thank you, that sounds like an interesting way to pass the time."

Trent frowned. "Why on earth do you want to see my offices?"

"Sheer, unadulterated curiosity, Trent," she explained. "Run along and shake hands with Mr. Baldwin." She swung around and walked out of the office. As she did so, Hal Reece's voice trailed clearly after her.

"I thought you were supposed to be on vacation, pal. Where in the world did you find her?"

"Out in the woods, living under a mushroom," Trent replied blandly.

"Never can tell what you'll find in those Oregon woods, can you?" Reece mused pleasantly.

Filomena wrinkled her nose and kept walking.

DINNER PROVED VERY ENJOYABLE. They ate in a posh downtown restaurant that featured seafood and pasta. Evelyn Reece was a charming, attractive woman in her early thirties who delighted in talking about her two young children. She and her husband were obviously very much in love, and they both seemed pleased to meet Filomena.

"I'm so happy you could come along, Fil," Evelyn said at one point, leaning confidentially across the table. "Trent doesn't get out nearly often enough these days. I'm always telling him he's never going to meet the woman of his dreams while he's sitting alone in his apartment working every night. Honestly, I thought it was women who needed to be encouraged to get out and meet their prospective mates, but I've learned men can be just as stubborn and reclusive."

"I resent that," Trent said mildly, his gaze on Filomena. "I am neither stubborn nor reclusive."

"Just picky, is that it?" Evelyn laughed. "Well, congratulations on finding yourself such a nice date for tonight. Does this mean I should give up my matchmaking efforts?"

"Yes, thank you, Evelyn. I would very much appreciate that." Trent spoke with so much depth of feeling that everyone, including Filomena, laughed.

Evelyn groaned and turned to Filomena for understanding. "I've tried, Fil, Lord knows I've tried. The man wants to get married. He needs to get married. It's written all over his face. But no luck."

"Uh, Evelyn," her husband said uneasily, his gaze flicking to Trent's impassive expression. "Fil probably isn't terribly interested in your past failures as a matchmaker. And neither is Trent."

"Nonsense," Evelyn said deliberately. "Fil ought to know what she's up against."

"I'm not up against anything, am I, Trent?" Filomena toyed with her wineglass and smiled at Trent, who regarded her with steady green eyes. "I'm just here to spend an evening away from all the peace and quiet of Gallant Lake."

"If you say so," he replied calmly, lifting his own wineglass.

She remembered what he had said about it being her decision where she would spend the night. So far she hadn't checked into a hotel; there hadn't been any time. She had changed for dinner in the ladies' room at the offices of Asgard Development. Trent had worn the same jacket and tie he had worn to the meeting with Baldwin. And with Hal Reece they had gone straight from Asgard to the restaurant, where Evelyn had been waiting.

But soon dinner would be over and then the decision could be delayed no longer. Filomena met Trent's eyes and felt herself drowning in the jade depths. The wineglass in her hand trembled.

"If you'll excuse me," Evelyn Reece announced lightly, "I'm going to take a trip to the ladies' room for a few emergency repairs. I'll be right back."

"I'll come with you," Filomena said, jumping to participate in the age-old feminine ritual of going in pairs to the rest room. She grabbed her purse.

Evelyn smiled and led the way through the crowded dining room. When they reached the marbled facilities, she grinned broadly and opened her bag to find her lipstick. She leaned toward the mirror to apply the lip color.

"I can't believe that after all my efforts Trent has finally found someone on his own. And in Gallant Lake, Oregon, no less. Although I must admit you don't look like you come from somewhere called Gallant Lake."

"You should have seen me nine years ago when I left the place," Filomena said with a chuckle as she ran a brush through her long hair.

"You said your business is headquartered in Seattle?"

"That's right."

"Will you be able to move your business down here to Portland, or is Trent going to have to move to Seattle?" Evelyn asked casually.

"What?" Filomena stared at her new friend in the mirror, stunned. "Why should either of us move?"

"Because I strongly suspect you're going to find yourselves married soon, and frankly, I can't see Trent in a commuting marriage. He's the kind of man who's going to want a strong, stable home life. He's waited for it long enough, and he deserves it. He was married once, you know, when he was in his early twenties. It was a disaster from what I understand. She left him for someone much older and much richer. Apparently she didn't realize just how successful Trent was going to become."

Filomena felt a wave of panic. "Please, no offense, Evelyn, but I assure you, you're jumping to conclusions. Trent and I have absolutely no permanent plans. We're simply friends."

"Sure, and if I believe that, you've got a bridge you can sell me, right?" Evelyn's eyes danced. "Come on, Fil, I've seen the way he looks at you. What's more, I'm in a position to compare that look with the way he's looked at half a dozen other women in the past year, and believe me, there's no comparison."

"Evelyn, please, I know you mean well but—"

"What I mean isn't nearly as important as what Trent means," Evelyn said bluntly. "The man wants to get married. Oh, he won't come right out and admit it, but I've watched him. He's been circling the available herd of females for eighteen months, looking for one to pair off with."

"You make him sound like a stag ready to mate."

"That's a pretty accurate description. For a while the hunt was fairly intense. He was dating a different woman every week. Then a few months ago he seemed to just give up. He stopped the heavy dating routine and started staying home more and more. I tried to fix him up a few times, but nothing ever clicked. Then he announced he was going to take off most of the summer and do some serious vacationing. Claimed he needed to get away for a while. The next thing we know he shows up with you and a look in his eyes that tells me the hunt is finally finished. What's this about him finding you under a mushroom?"

Filomena shivered slightly but struggled to keep her composure. She shook her head as she dropped her brush back into her bag. She decided to ignore the mushroom joke. "You're reading far too much into this, Evelyn, believe me."

"We'll see." Then she smiled reassuringly. "You don't have to be nervous, you know. Trent is one hundred percent for real. There's not a drop of falseness in the man. You can trust him to the ends of the earth. If he's serious about you, he'll make his intentions clear soon enough, and he'll stand by them."

Filomena's uneasiness grew. First her family had taken the attitude that she and Trent made an ideal couple. Now the Reeces appeared to have come to the same conclusion. As far as Filomena could tell, Trent wasn't doing anything to discourage the notion.

"Evelyn, I hate to disillusion you, but Trent has said nothing about marriage. He's said nothing about next week or next month, for that matter. To put it bluntly, I expect he's only looking for someone to entertain him while he stays at my parents' lodge. I landed on the doorstep a couple of weeks ago, and everyone, including Trent, seems to have decided it would be a good idea if he and I paired off together. It's difficult to explain, but there are reasons why everyone thinks it's such a nifty notion. And those reasons have nothing to do with a permanent relationship."

"I think you may be the one who's laboring under an illusion," Evelyn said lightly. "But don't worry about it. I expect Trent will make everything clear in his own good time."

There was no point in pursuing that topic, Filomena decided with a resigned sigh. But since Evelyn seemed chatty on the subject of Trent Ravinder, Filomena decided to try for an answer to a question that was beginning to bother her.

"Do you know why we drove all the way to Portland today, Evelyn?"

"Sure. Hal told me Baldwin was finally willing to sign the papers on that coast deal. Doesn't surprise me at all to learn he wouldn't do it without Trent present. Baldwin doesn't trust land developers."

"But he trusted Trent Ravinder?"

Evelyn grinned. "Your Mr. Ravinder is one of Asgard's greatest secret weapons. People trust him and will deal with him when they won't deal with anyone else. The man's as honest as the day is long, and his word is solid gold. Asgard uses him to negotiate deals no one else can close."

"What would happen if Trent made a promise on behalf of Asgard that wasn't carried out?" Filomena asked curiously.

"I doubt that could occur except by a genuine error. Old Asgard knows Trent would be gone in five minutes flat if something like that happened. He'll only work for Asgard as long as he knows Asgard will back him up. Asgard's biggest worry is that Trent will decide to go into business for himself one of these days, which is a distinct possibility."

"But how did Trent get such a reputation in the first place?"

"He earned it, I suppose," Evelyn said matter-of-factly. "And he defends it. He takes pride in it."

"I know," Filomena said slowly. "He can be very arrogant at times."

"If you want my opinion, I think something must have happened a long time ago, something that made Trent decide people would take him at his word or else."

"Hmm." Filomena gazed thoughtfully into the mirror.

Evelyn smiled back at her. "Better watch your step, Fil, especially if you're not sure you want to have him serious about you. Trent is famous for keeping his word come hell or high water. There's a corollary to that kind of reputation."

"What's that?"

"He always does what he sets out to do. The same pride and arrogance that makes it impossible for him to break his word also makes it impossible for him to be deflected from his goals. That particular talent has also made him useful to Asgard."

"I'll bet," Filomena replied. She wondered if she ought to just take to her heels right now before she got any more mired in Trent Ravinder's slowly closing trap.

But she hadn't run from anything since she'd fled from the scene of her fiancé in bed with another woman, Filomena reminded herself. She smiled at Evelyn, turned around and led the way to the door of the ladies' room. "Fortunately I'm quite fast on my feet," she murmured.

"You'll have to be to outrun Trent."

5

THE REMAINDER OF THE EVENING passed all too quickly. In no time at all, the Reeces were saying good-night on the sidewalk in front of the restaurant. They got into their car, waved and pulled away from the curb, leaving Filomena standing on the sidewalk next to Trent. He took her arm and started toward the Mercedes.

"Well, Filomena," Trent said a moment later as he slid into the driver's seat beside her, "have you made up your mind about where you want to spend the night?"

She felt her breath catch. It was supposed to be so easy. All she had to do was tell him he could take her to the nearest hotel and leave her there. Determinedly she cleared her throat. "It's been a lovely evening, Trent. I enjoyed meeting your friends. I think it would be best if you took me—"

"I'll take you to my apartment first," he interrupted smoothly, as though he'd figured out what she'd been about to say. "We can have a nightcap while you decide where you want to spend the night."

She blinked, recognizing defeat when she saw it. She knew what would happen if she went home with him. Still, she felt obligated to try to salvage some of her feminine independence.

"One nightcap," she said clearly. "And then you can take me to a hotel. I'll phone one from your apartment."

"If that's what you want." He spoke easily, apparently unconcerned with whatever she chose to do.

But Filomena knew otherwise. She could feel the tension in him. He appeared relaxed and at ease as he piloted the Mercedes through the downtown streets, but she sensed the hungry anticipation in him. It was easy to understand Evelyn Reece's likening Trent to a prowling male animal circling the herd until he found the female of his choice. Filomena knew now that he had been stalking her for the past two weeks. It alarmed her to realize she hadn't understood just how intent and serious he was about the whole thing until tonight. She stirred slightly in her seat.

"You're not going to panic now, are you?" Trent asked conversationally as he guided the Mercedes into the underground parking garage of a modern high rise.

"Why should I panic?" Filomena asked aggressively. She wished he didn't find it so easy to read her mind.

"Because you're finally starting to focus on me, and you're realizing that you can't keep dancing just out of reach. It's time to stand still and face me."

"What's that supposed to mean?"

"For the past two weeks I've had to compete with everything from an old flame to a houseful of your relatives. On top of that, you've been only paying scant attention to me because you've been having so much fun causing a sensation in Gallant Lake. But tonight you're on your own, aren't you? No family to use as an excuse for going home early. No one around to be impressed by your flashy Porsche and your one-of-a-kind clothes. No outrageous parties to give. There simply aren't any more distractions to put in my path. Tonight it's just you and me."

"Is that a threat?" Filomena asked, trying to remain calm.

He smiled at her as he pulled into a parking space and switched off the ignition. The curve of his mouth was enigmatic, but the garage lighting revealed the watchful brilliance in his eyes. "No, Filomena, it's not a threat. Just a statement of fact. There's nowhere to run tonight. You have to deal with me. One way or another, you have to make some decisions about us."

Her chin came up with a touch of defiance. "And if I'm not ready to make any decisions?"

He regarded her in silence for a long moment and then he opened his door. "You're ready. You just don't want to admit it." He got out of the car and came around to open her door. "Come on, honey. Let's go upstairs and decide where you're going to spend the night."

She got out of the car without a word, drawn by a magnetism that was too strong to resist. Filomena could feel the satisfaction in Trent. It radiated from him. He was sure that two weeks of patient hunting had finally paid off. All of the way up to the twenty-second floor in the elevator, Filomena reminded herself that she didn't have to stay unless she wanted to. She could have the promised drink and then leave. She could call a cab. She could insist Trent drive her to a hotel. In a pinch, she could walk.

She was still giving herself that reassuring pep talk when she walked through the door of his apartment. Curiosity took over immediately, banishing her uncertainties. This was the same sort of curiosity she had experienced that afternoon when she'd walked through his offices. There she had found cool, clean, utilitarian lines and shapes and forms, evidence of a man who worked hard and efficiently, a man who did not like his office environment cluttered up with frills and amenities.

"Well?" Trent asked in amusement as he watched her walk across the gray carpet, "is it what you were expecting?" He closed the door, locked it and then leaned against it as he followed her progress around the living room.

"I think so," Filomena said slowly as she examined the functional, comfortable furnishings. "Yes, it's exactly what I was expecting." It was a room that had been designed for a man's comfort and convenience, a *large* man's comfort and convenience. The furniture seemed oversized to her, rather like the furniture in her parents' house. The leather and wood were expensive but not flashy, modern but not high tech.

"I'll bet it's a lot different than your apartment," Trent observed. He came away from the door and headed toward the kitchen.

Filomena trailed after him, intrigued. "What do you think my place looks like?"

He shrugged as he opened a cupboard door and took down a bottle of brandy. "Oh, probably lots of delicate, sleek, modern stuff. Glossy, trendy, eye-catching. The sort of stuff that would probably collapse if anyone larger than a jockey sat in it. Not especially comfortable but definitely state of the art."

She smiled to herself at the accuracy of his description. "You sound disapproving."

He shook his head. "No. You have a strong interest in design. It makes sense you'd indulge that interest in your own apartment. Nothing wrong with that." He poured the brandy and handed her a glass.

Filomena took it, still smiling faintly. "You're wrong about one thing. My furniture is not uncomfortable. At least, not for me," she amended, glancing from the top of his head to the toes of his leather shoes. "It's possible that someone of your size and height might find it a bit cramped, though."

"You must be feeling desperate if you're resorting to cracks about my size." Trent took a sip of his brandy.

"I heard you making cracks about my height to your friend Hal Reece this afternoon."

"Such as?" Trent asked politely.

"Something about finding me living under a mushroom out in the woods, I believe."

He grinned, not the least abashed. "Ah, that. Well, I'll admit there's something about you that reminds me of an elf, and it isn't just your size."

"No?"

"No, it's the fact that you have a talent for creating mischief."

"I resent that," Filomena said lightly. "I do not go around causing mischief. I've got better things to do with my time."

"Perhaps when you're working in the offices of Cromwell & Sterling you do, but when you're on vacation I'm not so sure. If you want my opinion, your entire family was grateful to me this afternoon when I offered to get you out of town for a while."

Filomena couldn't stifle the burst of laughter that rose within her. "Have I really succeeded in making everyone so nervous?"

"Yes, and you enjoyed every minute of it, didn't you?"

Filomena's laughter faded. "I didn't enjoy that phone call from Gloria Paxton this afternoon," she confessed with a sigh. She turned away, walking slowly back into the living room.

"I'm glad she called," Trent surprised her by saying as he followed her.

Filomena frowned at him over her shoulder. "You are?"

"Sure." He reached out and flicked a wall switch that turned off the lights. A soft, velvety darkness descended on the room. "If Gloria hadn't called when she did," he went on softly, "it might have been a lot harder to talk you into coming to Portland with me."

Filomena stood unmoving in the shadows. She tried to concentrate on the lights of the city below her, but the only thing she was really conscious of was the knowledge that Trent was almost upon her. He moved quietly, she thought, all silent grace and sleek male strength. A prowling male looking for a mate. And he wanted her.

"But you would have tried to talk me into the trip, anyway?" she asked in a whisper.

He stopped directly behind her. His hand touched her shoulder, his palm warm and large and strong. The feel of him burned through the turquoise silk of her dress. "Would it have been so hard to convince you to come with me?"

She hesitated and then turned slowly to face him. "I don't know," she admitted honestly.

Trent gently removed the glass from her hand and set it down beside his own on a nearby table. Then he slowly pushed his fingers into the depths of her fiery hair. "Are you sure?" He lowered his head until his forehead was resting against hers. "Are you sure you don't know the answer, Filomena?"

"Is it important?"

"I want to be sure you know what you're doing."

She trembled as his fingers traced small, random circles on the nape of her neck. "I seem to be doing what you want me to do. Isn't that enough?" she demanded softly.

"No."

"What do you want from me?" She felt slightly desperate.

He tilted her chin with his thumbs and brushed his mouth against hers. "I need to hear you say you want me. I've seen hints of it in your eyes, in the way you tease me by staying just out of reach, in the way you kissed me last night. But I want to hear the words. Is that simple and straightforward enough for you, Filomena?"

"Yes."

"Then tell me," he ordered softly, his thumbs stroking her jaw in a slow, deliciously hypnotic manner. His eyes had been made colorless by the absence of light, but no shadow could dim the gleam of masculine desire in his gaze as he looked down at her.

"I...I want you, Trent." The words came out in a rush before Filomena could stop them. She bit her lip, wishing she could have called back the confession, but it was too late. And it wouldn't have made much difference anyway, she thought with a flash of unnerving insight. He already *knew*. He was only making her say the words so that they would both know.

"Thank you, Filomena. I swear you won't regret it." He covered her mouth with his own, his breath a sighing groan of need and rising desire.

Filomena felt his hands slide down her shoulders, and then his arms were around her, locking her to him as he kissed her with slow, drugging thoroughness. The strength and heat of him reached out to engulf her. She was trapped, not just by his physical size and power, but by something far more insidious. Filomena couldn't put a name to the emotion that held her in a grip as unshakable as Trent's arms, but it made her wary. For a moment or two she experienced a flare of panic. It warred with the flames of passion that were uncurling inside her, and Trent seemed to sense it.

"You're not afraid of me," he said against her soft mouth.

"No." Her nails sank into his shirt.

"Are you afraid of yourself?" It was a challenge.

"No!"

"Then stop fighting both of us. I'm going to make love to you tonight, and I don't want you thinking about anything else but that. Most of all I don't want you thinking of escape."

She tipped her head back and met his gaze. He was filling her senses and her mind tonight. All of the excuses and distractions she had been using for the past two weeks to avoid this moment had dissolved into mist. Tonight there was nothing else to cling to except Trent. She couldn't think of anything else except him, didn't want anything else except him.

For a moment they stared at each other and then, with a soft murmur of surrender, Filomena rested her head on Trent's shoulder. She trembled as he lifted his hand to stroke her hair.

Filomena never knew how long they stood there in the shadows. She realized that Trent was deliberately not rushing her now that he had won her acceptance of the attraction that existed between them.

"I want you to get used to this," he said quietly as he continued to hold her close. "I want you to learn the feel of me, the feel of being in my arms. I want you to know this is where you belong."

Filomena stirred against him, putting her hand on his chest. He smelled good, she thought. Very male and very sexy. She opened her eyes and found herself staring at the buttons on his shirt. Without even thinking about it, she slid her fingers to the first one and pried it free. Trent drew in his breath but said nothing.

When he didn't move or try to push matters along any more swiftly, Filomena grew bolder. She undid another of his shirt buttons and slipped her fingers inside the opening to find the rough, curling hair on his chest.

Trent's hand twisted urgently in her hair and then Filomena felt him force himself to relax. The realization that he was deliberately restraining himself warmed her. She pushed aside the fabric of his shirt and dropped a tiny kiss on his chest.

"Sweetheart," he muttered in a dark voice filled with gathering passion. "I want you so badly it's eating me alive." He groaned as he lowered his mouth to hers once more.

Filomena sighed deeply and opened herself to him both physically and mentally. This was what she wanted tonight. She was through with the game of hide-and-seek she had been consciously and unconsciously playing for the past two weeks. Tonight she longed to explore the emotions and the passions she had been deliberately keeping at bay.

She murmured his name, heard him groan again and then she felt the exciting slide of his tongue along the edge of her lips. A second later he was inside, claiming her mouth with an intimacy and aggression that foreshadowed the other claim he would soon make.

When Trent broke the heavy kiss at last, it was to find the gentle curve of her shoulder. Filomena closed her eyes as he tasted her skin with the tantalizing edge of his tongue. She leaned into his warmth, no longer shying from the size and strength of him. Tonight that size and strength promised passion and excitement, unlike anything she had ever known. She pushed herself closer to him, her hands circling his neck, her breasts crushed against his chest.

"This is the way I've wanted you," Trent muttered. "For days I've been torturing myself with thoughts of you clinging like this."

"I want you," she whispered, unable to say anything else. She felt dazed with the need for him.

"I know, darling," Trent said with soft satisfaction. "I know." He found the buttons at the back of her dress and undid them with slow, deliberate movements. A moment later the turquoise silk slid from her shoulders, down to her hips and then crumpled into a soft pool on the carpet. When she stepped out of it, she also stepped out of her shoes.

Filomena felt suddenly very vulnerable in Trent's arms. She had on only a lacy scrap of bra, a pair of panty hose and tiny silken panties. She buried her face against his shirt when his fingers freed the snaps of the small bra. When it fell to the floor at his feet, Filomena couldn't stifle a small cry that was part anticipation, part wariness.

"You want this, honey," he whispered as he slid his palms down over the curve of her breasts. "You want it as much as I do."

She felt her nipples tightening into hard buds of desire under his hands. "I know," she admitted.

"Prove it," he said with a slight smile. "Show me how much you want me tonight."

She saw the challenge in the smile, but she also saw something else. Beneath the masculine provocation there was another, deeper message. He needed to know how much she wanted him tonight. Filomena couldn't deny him the proof he sought.

Slowly, with fingers that shook slightly, she began undoing the rest of the buttons on his shirt. When the last had been freed, she pushed the garment from his shoulders. It fell to the carpet alongside her dress.

"Come here," Trent said thickly. His hands slid down her back and curved under her bottom. He lifted her easily until her breasts were on a level with his mouth. Filomena's fingernails dug into his shoulders as he tasted first one throbbing peak and then the other. She gasped as he let her slide slowly back down the length of him. The hair on his chest teased her nipples as she was lowered slowly to her feet.

She looked up at him from under her lashes. "I suppose there are some advantages to your size."

His smile was brief, sexy and wicked. "I've been wanting to do that for a long time. There are definitely some advantages to your size. Very convenient."

"Such as?" she demanded.

"Well, for example, I can pick you up in one hand."

"I'm not that small or that light!"

"Want to bet?" He slid one arm around her waist and lifted her easily up against him again. With his free hand he drew a circle around one of her nipples.

Filomena gave him a rueful grimace and then she laughed softly. She thrust her fingers into his hair and pressed herself closer. "You win," she said huskily.

"Do I?" There was an unexpected seriousness in his eyes as he set her back down on her feet.

She wanted to ask him what he meant by that, but he wasn't waiting for an answer to the enigmatic question. Instead he slid his fingers under the waistband of her panty hose and pushed the hose and her panties quickly down over her hips. An instant later Filomena was completely naked. She stood in the circle of his arms and looked up at him.

"You're so small and graceful," he murmured wonderingly. "So light and soft and delicate." He shook his head slowly and ran his hands down her waist to her hips. "And you've kept me dangling so long."

"No, not deliberately. I just wasn't sure." Anxiously she tried to explain. "And it hasn't been a long time. Only two weeks."

"The longest two weeks of my life," he assured her. "But now the waiting is over." He moved, lowering her to the carpet. Then he knelt on one knee beside her, his hands impatiently at work on his belt buckle.

When he shoved aside his slacks and briefs, Filomena stared at him, drinking in the solid planes of his body. She put out a hand and touched his muscled thigh. Her eyes lifted to his. "No one could ever accuse you of being elf size," she whispered tremulously.

"I'll assume that's a compliment," he said with a soft chuckle.

Then he was lowering himself alongside her on the carpet, exploring her with his hands and his mouth and occasionally, excitingly, with his teeth. His leg moved over hers, sliding between her thighs and forcing them gently apart.

Filomena felt as if she were being inundated by a huge, breaking wave. She no longer had any thoughts of resistance or caution or even of the future. All she wanted, all she longed for in this moment was Trent's touch. She could no longer even imagine why she had been trying to stay clear of such exquisite involvement. She clutched at him, urging his mouth back to hers when he would have spent more time in the vicinity of her belly button.

"What is it, Filomena?" he asked. But there was a knowing look in his eyes as he stretched out alongside her again.

"I was just wondering why I waited so long," she said honestly. Her palms moved over his shoulders, enjoying the hard feel of contoured muscle and bone. She twisted against him and felt the throbbing heat of his manhood brush along her thigh.

"That's a good question. Unfortunately it doesn't have a good answer." Trent flattened his palm on her stomach and drew his hand lower. His fingers clenched briefly in the small, soft triangle at the apex of her legs and then he was exploring even lower. His touch became excruciatingly intimate.

Filomena sucked in her breath, dizzy with sensation as Trent found the liquid warmth between her thighs. She heard his groan of desire and shivered in his grasp. He held her more tightly.

"The waiting is over, for both of us," he muttered as he widened the space between her legs with his hand.

She had no response to that. She doubted if she could have said anything very coherent at all in that moment. She felt him moving, lifting himself and then coming down on top of her. His arms went around her, cradling her as he began to crush her into the carpet.

"Look at me, Filomena," Trent ordered in a thick, hoarse voice as he positioned himself. "I want to see your eyes when I make you mine this first time."

She obeyed, unable to look away as he pressed himself against her. She felt the hard, thrusting pressure between her legs and instinctively lifted her hips to receive him.

"*Trent.*"

He responded by pushing forward relentlessly. His fingers tightened on her skin. Slowly, inevitably, he filled her with himself.

Filomena's eyes did close then, squeezing shut as Trent entered her. The moment of union was almost overwhelming. Her whole body tightened to a point just short of pain in response to the intrusion. Trent was a large man, and she'd had very little experience with men in a physical sense.

But a glittering, intoxicating excitement followed rapidly on the heels of the initial reaction.

It was unlike anything Filomena had ever experienced. When she opened her eyes again, Trent was looking down at her. He didn't move for a long moment, giving her a chance to adjust to the feel of him deep inside her.

"I've never felt anything like this before in my life." Trent flexed his hips slowly, withdrawing an inch or so and then carefully retracing his path so that he was once again deep inside her.

"No," Filomena managed, dimly aware that she was clutching at him. "Neither have I."

"Don't you think I can tell? I can see it in your eyes, feel it in your body. I knew we were going to be good together. I knew it the moment I met you." He buried his face in the curve of her neck and began to move again, this time establishing a slow, sensual rhythm that sent tremors of excitement through Filomena.

"Oh, Trent . . ."

"Hold on to me, sweetheart. Hold on to me and never let go. We'll find it together, I promise."

He was right. That was the thing about Trent Ravinder, Filomena told herself, you could count on him. He knew where he was taking her. He led the way, making sure she kept up with him all along the route.

The pattern of excitement swirled outward, encompassing both of them. Filomena had never explored this kind of sensation before in her life. She was old enough and sophisticated enough to know she had missed out on something, but there had been too many other things going on in her world to let it worry her. Or perhaps there had simply never been a man in her life who could make it worthwhile to worry about such matters. Whatever the reason, the explosive climax that was the final culmination in lovemaking burst upon her with unexpected force.

"Yes, sweetheart, *yes*. Take it. Hold on to it. Hold on to me." He drove himself into her one last time as her satisfaction pulled him over the edge. His hoarse shout of triumph and pleasure echoed in the dark room, mingling with Filomena's panting, breathless cries.

And then they were falling together through the slackening currents, collapsing in a tangle of perspiration-dampened arms and legs.

"Trent, I didn't know..." Filomena tried to find the words through a languid haze. "I didn't realize it could be like this."

"I know," he soothed, stroking long strands of her hair back from her face. "I didn't realize it, either."

"I thought you said you knew." She lifted her lashes and smiled dreamily up at him.

He grinned faintly. "I said I knew it would be good. I didn't know how good."

"Hah. I thought you knew everything."

"Not quite. Not about you."

"Well, thank goodness for that," she said decisively. She curled into his arms and planted a small kiss on his chest. "A woman is entitled to a few secrets."

His eyes grew serious again as he looked down at her. "I don't want there to be any secrets between us, Filomena. I want us to know each other so well that we have no secrets. Do you understand?"

Her fingers drifted across his chest as a sudden thought occurred to her. "Do you want to tell me your secrets?"

"What do you want to know?"

She drew a deep breath and took the plunge. "Well, for starters, I'd like to know why you have this thing about trust."

He frowned. "What thing?"

"You know what I mean," she said slowly. "You're very arrogant about your...your sense of honor, the fact that your word is your bond and all that. Why is it such a big deal with you, Trent?"

"Most people want others to respect them. I don't see what's so strange about my feelings on the subject."

She smiled gently. "You said no secrets, remember? But you've got a few, don't you?"

He lay on his back, one arm folded under his head, looking up at the ceiling for a long time. One knee was drawn up as he absently stroked her hair and shoulder. "I guess it has something to do with the way I was raised," he said finally.

"Your parents were strict?" she ventured.

He laughed shortly. "No, it wasn't that. My father died when I was a baby. My mother remarried before I was two, and I grew up thinking of my mother's second husband as my father."

"Was he a good man?" Filomena asked hesitantly, beginning to wonder if she'd had any right to pry. It was obviously a difficult subject for Trent.

"I thought so until I was eight."

"What happened then?"

"He was arrested for embezzlement at the bank where he worked. They sent him to prison for a couple of years."

"How awful for you and your mother."

"It was bad because we lived in a small town. Everyone knew what had happened, and no one let my mother or me forget it for a single moment." Trent's voice hardened. "Whenever anything was missing out of someone's desk at school, the finger usually got pointed at me. Storekeepers kept a sharp eye on me whenever I came through the doors in case I had inherited any of Dad's light-fingered tendencies. Whenever I got into trouble there was almost always someone around to say, 'Like father, like son.'"

"I think I get the picture," Filomena said unhappily.

"When Dad got out of prison, things didn't get much better. We finally had to move. It was difficult for him to get a job and harder for him to keep it. Sooner or later someone would find out about his past, and the next thing I knew I was in a fight at school or out in a parking lot trying to shut someone's mouth the hard way."

"I'll bet you won most of those fights." Filomena's heart went out to an embattled boy struggling desperately to defend the family honor.

He shrugged. "Winning didn't change anyone's opinion or make them stop talking."

"So you grew up determined to compensate for your father's weakness, is that it? You made sure everyone knew you weren't the same kind of man he was. Whatever happens, you can be trusted and everyone else had damn well better be honest with you or you'll demolish them, right?"

His mouth curved slightly as he raised himself on his elbow and regarded her with a thoughtful expression. "Something like that."

She searched his face. "Aren't you afraid at times that you might be a little too, well, rigid about it? I mean it's all well and good to be noble about this sort of thing, but not everyone can live up to your standards, Trent."

"Honesty is a clear-cut, black-and-white issue, Filomena. There's no room for gray areas "

"That's a harsh way to view things."

He shrugged. "I'm not gullible. I won't be played for a fool, and I definitely won't let someone get away with taking advantage of me. If that strikes you as overly rigid and harsh, well, that's too bad. It's the way I am."

Filomena gnawed on her lower lip as she considered that. "Does it happen often? Someone trying to take advantage of you, I mean."

His expression turned sardonic. "What do you think?"

She shook her head. "I don't think it does."

"Maybe that only goes to prove that if you treat people fairly, they'll treat you that way in return."

"I doubt it," Filomena said. "I think what it proves is that people are probably scared to death to mess with you."

"Either way, it works," he said equably. "Very few people try to cheat me or play me for a fool."

"I'll bet," Filomena said with great depth of feeling.

6

FILOMENA OPENED HER EYES to sunlight and a strange room. She lay perfectly still for a moment, clinging to the very edge of the wide bed. Without turning to look she knew Trent was lying beside her. There was nothing magic about the realization; she could feel his weight putting a definite dent in the center of the king-size mattress. She could also feel the warmth of him under the covers. Sleeping with a man of Trent's size, she discovered, was like sleeping with a large bear. He provided enough heat for both of them. The thought made her smile.

"Do you always wake up smiling?" Trent asked through a hearty yawn.

"Nope."

"Good. A little of that kind of thing goes a long way in the mornings." He chuckled lazily and reached out to tumble her back across the mattress until she was curled next to him. "What are you doing over on that side of the bed? How did you get away from me in the middle of the night, anyway? When I went to sleep I had you right here by my side."

"I was afraid I'd get crushed," she said half-seriously.

"The hell you were. You just aren't used to sleeping with someone." He patted her rear with a casual, proprietary gesture. "But that's all right. You'll get accustomed to it."

"I take it you are accustomed to it?" she asked before she could stop herself.

She sensed rather than saw his slow grin. "Are we at the stage where you start asking pointed questions about my past relationships?"

Filomena cleared her throat. "Uh, I don't think I want to hear about your past relationships."

"Coward."

"I prefer to think of myself as discreet."

He pretended to give that considerable thought. "Okay, I'll go along with that. Discreet, it is. You're a surprisingly rational, pragmatic, levelheaded, intelligent female, for an elf."

Filomena was silent for a long moment and then she asked very cautiously, "Have you had a lot of relationships?"

Trent roared with laughter, moving abruptly to pin her beneath him. "So much for discreet, rational, pragmatic, levelheaded and intelligent, huh?"

"I resent that. I am definitely intelligent."

"All right, I'll give you that. The answer to your idiotic question, Filomena Cromwell, is no, there haven't been a lot of relationships in my past. And certainly none that were anywhere near as important as the one I have with you." He paused and then went on more seriously. "I was married once. It didn't last very long. She didn't want to wait for me to make it to the top. Found someone else who was already there. End of story." His expression relaxed once more. "Well? How's that for discretion?"

"I'm glad you don't apply your honesty-is-the-best-policy to every little thing," she murmured. She really didn't want to know too much about the women in his past, especially the one he had married.

To her surprise, he took the comment seriously. "I swear I will always be honest with you, sweetheart, but there are some things that don't concern us. I'm an advocate of the truth, but that doesn't mean I believe that everything has to be dredged up out of the past and rehashed. Satisfied?"

She nodded. "I'm satisfied."

He drew his hand over her hip and squeezed gently, clearly enjoying the feel of her. "Now that we've agreed the past can be more or less consigned to oblivion, let's talk about the future."

For some reason his words sent a wave of uneasiness through her, the first she had experienced since surrendering to his lovemaking last night. Filomena pushed the trickle of alarm aside and smiled boldly up at him. "What about the future?"

"On second thought," he murmured, pausing to drop a kiss in the hollow of her throat, "I don't think there's any need to rush that discussion. We've got plenty of time." He dropped another teasing kiss, this time on the upper swell of her breast.

Filomena relaxed. "I agree. No need to rush into that particular conversation."

He lifted his head and eyed her quizzically. "You sound as if someone just granted you a reprieve. I thought women were very big on discussions of the future."

"We have a lot to learn about each other, Trent," she pointed out. "The future will take care of itself. It always does."

"No," he said with a faint edge to his voice, "the future doesn't always take care of itself. But in this case, you don't have to worry about it too much."

"Why?"

"Because I'll be taking care of it for you."

Her sense of uneasiness returned in a rush. "Trent, maybe we should have that discussion now. I think we ought to get things clear between us, don't you? I mean, we hardly know each other, and I wouldn't want either of us to get any false impressions or wrong ideas or—"

He silenced her with a brief, possessive kiss. When he raised his head, his eyes were very green in the morning light. "Don't panic, elf. You're in good hands."

She felt those hands moving on her, parting her legs and exploring the sensitive skin of her inner thigh. Her arms went around his neck, and the future receded. "Yes," she whispered, tugging his head back down to hers, "I'm very definitely in good hands."

TRENT COULD SENSE the difference in the atmosphere between himself and Filomena from the moment they awoke that morning. Her awareness of him had exploded into full bloom at last. He could see it in her eyes and feel it in her touch. She was finally within reach, he thought. He'd managed to lure her close enough to the flame to ensure she felt its compelling pull.

The task was far from over, though, he reminded himself during the drive to Gallant Lake. But the hard part, the trickiest part, had been accomplished. He could afford to relax a little now and watch Filomena explore her new feelings toward him.

She was still nervous, still uncertain, but already the barriers were tumbling. Trent could tell that at odd moments she would realize that things were changing quickly for her, and the knowledge worried her. He could also see the occasional bemusement in her eyes.

But most of the time she ignored her fears and concentrated on the intriguing pleasure she was learning to enjoy around him. Filomena Cromwell, Trent thought, was discovering what falling in love was all about. At least, he added, mentally crossing his fingers, he hoped that was what she was discovering.

"What are you thinking about?" Filomena asked cheerfully at one point on the drive back to Gallant Lake.

He smiled faintly, his eyes on the traffic ahead. "I'm thinking that I've finally got your attention."

For some reason she seemed to find that hilariously amusing. She laughed for the next mile.

Trent wasn't the only one who noticed the difference in Filomena. When they arrived in Gallant Lake, her whole family sensed the change in the relationship almost immediately. Trent saw the warm humor and the undeniable expression of relief in their eyes. At dinner that night the conversation inevitably got around to the trip to Portland. Filomena was surprisingly vocal on the subject.

"Hal Reece and his wife were quite charming," she said chattily as she helped herself to salad. "We had a lovely dinner after Trent finished his business. Evelyn Reece apologized to me for her husband having to drag Trent away from his vacation, but there was obviously no alternative. Mr. Baldwin refused to sign on the dotted line until he had shaken Trent's hand over the deal. Evelyn told me that happens a lot. Asgard uses Trent to wrap up the big ones because people trust him. They'll deal with him when they won't deal with anyone else."

"I see," Amery said, his half amused, half speculative gaze on Trent who was calmly making his way through a thick chunk of sourdough bread. "Is that your main job with Asgard? Closing the tough ones?"

Trent shook his head. "No, that's just part of it. I do a lot of what I guess you'd call troubleshooting. I'm the one who gets sent out when things start going wrong on a deal or a job site. I think Asgard sees me as a sort of handyman."

"Don't let him give you any false impressions," Filomena declared. "He's got an office three times the size of mine. It's got a spectacular view and wall-to-wall carpeting. He's even got his own secretary. Companies such as Asgard don't reward their handymen with huge corner offices and private secretaries unless they are very, *very* handy."

Trent realized that Filomena was the only one at the table who seemed unaware of the pride in her voice. He was shocked to feel a faint warmth in his face as she continued singing his praises to her family. He was also acutely aware of the fact that it was all everyone could do to stifle smiles. He didn't know whether to laugh or groan, but he decided he'd better find a way to change the subject before she managed to thoroughly embarrass him.

"Filomena," he began gently when he found a slight pause in her monologue.

" . . . and Evenlyn Reece also told me that Asgard is willing to back up any promise Trent makes to a client because the company doesn't dare take the risk of losing him . . ."

"Filomena . . ."

"I met Mr. Asgard himself after the meeting. He told Trent he 'owed him one.' Wasn't that how he put it, Trent? Said he couldn't have closed the deal without you, and he wanted that land very much."

Trent cleared his throat. "Filomena, would you please pass me the potatoes?"

"Of course." She reached for the potatoes and started to tell her family about the view from Trent's office windows. "You can see the river and most of the bridges."

"Filomena," Trent tried again, putting more force into his voice. "How about another helping of vegetables?"

"Oh, no thanks, I've had enough." She smiled brilliantly at him and went off on another tangent. "Evelyn and Hal Reece hinted that Trent is probably going to become a partner in the firm one of these days unless he decides to leave and start his own company. Reece said Asgard is terrified of that possibility and will probably do anything to keep him."

"*Filomena.*"

She broke off expectantly. "Yes, Trent?"

"I think," he said firmly, "your family might appreciate a change of topic. I know I would."

She blinked at him and then comprehension flooded her expression. Her cheeks turned a light pink. "Oh, dear, was I embarrassing you, Trent?"

"That's putting it mildly."

She grinned. "You should have kicked me under the table."

"I was considering it," he admitted.

"Afraid I might have kicked you back?"

"The thought occurred to me, but I was getting desperate."

"Poor man. All right, the field is yours," she declared, waving a hand to include the entire spectrum of human conversation. "Pick a subject, any subject."

"Fishing," Trent said, turning to Amery with a sense of relief.

His host accommodated him immediately, but not before Trent had seen the amused satisfaction in Amery's eyes. Meg and Shari were eyeing Filomena with the same expression. Only Filomena seemed blissfully unaware of how much she had just revealed about her feelings for Trent.

Trent decided he could put up with some dinner-table embarrassment in exchange for those revelations. When Filomena finally started falling in love, she did so with considerable enthusiasm.

During the next three days, Trent basked in Filomena's awakening emotions. Her newfound awareness of him was expressed in a variety of ways. For example, two days after the return from Portland he came back from a morning's fishing expedition with two beautiful trout. Amery had been unable to accompany him that morning, so Trent had gone alone. It was Filomena who jumped up from the breakfast table where she had been lingering over her coffee with her sister and offered to fry the catch.

"The kitchen is very busy this morning," she explained, taking the fish from him. She headed toward the swinging doors that divided the kitchen from the dining area. "I'll take care of these for you."

Trent caught Shari's astonished look as he sat down across from her and reached for the coffee. He smiled blandly in return. "Something wrong, Shari?"

"I can't believe it," Shari murmured dryly. "I think she wants to show you she can cook."

Trent grinned. "Can she?"

"Oh, yes. Mother made sure we both learned how to do a decent job in the kitchen. She has old-fashioned ideas about what makes a woman marriageable. Not that those ideas have done Fil much good. Lately we'd all begun to wonder if Fil might have actually meant what she said nine years ago when she left town."

Trent sipped his coffee. "What did she say nine years ago?"

Shari lifted one shoulder. "A lot of things we didn't think she meant at the time."

"Things about not ever getting married?"

Shari smiled slightly. "Something like that. She would never admit it, but the truth is, she was badly shaken by the way her engagement ended. If Brady had just told her he wanted out of the arrangement, it wouldn't have been so bad. Fil could have handled that with a few tears and some sighs. Instead, she had to walk in and find him in bed with Gloria Halsey. Gloria was Fil's nemesis all through high school. She was the opposite of Fil in so many ways. Homecoming Queen, cheerleader, most popular girl in the class. You know the type. And she wasn't an especially nice person. She had a tendency to make fun of Fil."

"Do you think Filomena was in love with Brady?"

"Filomena was infatuated with him, but I don't think she was really in love with him. She was too young and too naive in many ways for that. She'd never even had a real boyfriend before Brady. He was the first man who had ever paid much attention to her, and she was starved for masculine attention. When Brady started courting her, she was thrilled."

"Why did Brady start chasing her if he preferred the Gloria Halsey type?"

Shari considered that carefully. "I've wondered about that myself a few times. It might have had something to do with the fact that Fil was finally starting to come out of her cocoon that first year in college. She began losing weight and became more sociable. She developed a lot of new interests in school and began to gain some confidence. She came home on weekends and vacations that first year, and Brady had just returned to town after graduating from college. He probably noticed the changes. Or maybe he was just bored. There weren't a lot of single women around, and Gloria was involved with someone else at the time and rarely came home from school. It's a small town. Brady didn't have a lot to choose from on Saturday night."

"So he just started hanging around with Filomena, is that it?"

"Yes. I'm sure his ego got a boost out of the association. She adored him, and it showed. And then, before anyone had quite realized how serious it all was, they announced their engagement. Filomena was on cloud nine. Meanwhile, Gloria came back for the summer. She was free and bored, and she decided she wanted Brady. Brady decided he wanted Gloria and a partnership in her father's insurance business. But I guess he had a little trouble figuring out how to break the news to my sister."

"So he let her find out the hard way." Trent heard the rough edge in his voice and deliberately tried to blunt it.

Shari nodded. "Poor kid. It was a terrible way to learn that a lot of men can't be trusted. I'm afraid she took the lesson to heart. She has no feeling left for Brady, but she never quite got over the lesson he taught her. She left town swearing she would never marry." Shari's mouth curved slightly. "My mother has been waiting nine years for her to change her mind."

"But instead of changing her mind about marriage and men, Filomena has devoted herself to founding Cromwell & Sterling," Trent concluded.

"Not entirely," Shari said slowly. "She does seem to have a very active social life in Seattle."

"I was afraid of that," Trent said with a groan. "She's got money of her own, style and flash. That would buy anyone an active social life."

"True, but she's never gotten involved enough with any man to consider a permanent relationship. These days she has to worry about fortune hunters, you know.

Cromwell & Sterling is growing by leaps and bounds. There are plenty of men out there who wouldn't mind having a piece of the action. So, what with one thing and another, Fil has learned to keep men at a distance. I don't think she's even aware of doing it most of the time."

"I know." Trent wasn't aware of how much feeling he'd put into the words until he saw Shari smiling. "What's so funny?"

"Nothing, really. It's just that, as I suspected all along, when Fil's barriers started to collapse, they did so in a big way. She's a changed woman since you brought her back from Portland, Trent. I've never seen her like this with anyone. If she isn't in love with you yet, she's getting there in a hurry."

Trent kept his smile noncommittal even though his body was growing tight with a combination of desire and fierce satisfaction. "Do you think so?"

"Oh, yes," Shari said quietly, "I think so. Is that what you really want, Trent? Because if it's not, please don't take this any farther. It wouldn't be fair to Fil, and frankly, I think the family would be awfully upset if you hurt her badly."

Trent gave Shari a level look. "You have my word of honor I have no intention of hurting your sister. I want her. My main goal right now is to make her want me."

Shari held his gaze for a long while and then she nodded, satisfied. "I believe you." Her expression lightened. "I think you're well on your way to accomplishing your goal."

Trent raised his eyebrows as he took another sip of coffee. "Knowing Filomena, it won't be that easy."

"You're probably right." Shari leaned back in her chair, contemplating him with sisterly concern. "Right now everything is peaches and cream, isn't it? But what's going to happen the first time you two argue? I'd better warn you that Fil doesn't take orders from any man, and she usually gets her own way when the chips are down."

"I'm not surprised," Trent said equably.

"So what happens the first time you put your foot down?" Shari asked with great interest. "She's become very independent during these past few years. She's her own woman. And even though she keeps it under control these days, she has a temper to go with that red hair. No matter how much you want her, I don't see you letting her run roughshod over you."

Trent chuckled. "That's a funny image. A redheaded elf running roughshod over me. She'd probably wear cleated boots to do the job right."

"Probably. So?"

Trent sighed. "So what will happen the first time I put my foot down? I'm not sure. But there's one thing in my favor."

"What's that?"

"I have very big feet."

AT THE BEGINNING of the third day back after the fateful trip to Portland, Filomena began to get impatient. She'd had almost no time at all alone with Trent. Even more annoying was the fact that he didn't seem to be going out of his way to create any time for the two of them to be together.

It didn't make sense. For the first couple of weeks of their relationship he had concentrated on finding ways to get her alone. She had had her hands full trying to avoid such encounters. Now Trent appeared to be content to share her with her family.

She had a few anxious moments when it had occurred to her that, having gotten her into bed once, he'd lost all interest in repeating the experience. Whenever these doubts struck, however, she would invariably look up to find him watching her with those jade eyes of his, and she'd know in her bones that he still wanted her.

So why wasn't he making more of an effort to find a time and place to make love to her? she wondered in growing annoyance. It would be simple enough. He could take her for a drive in the evening, or invite her on a walk down by the lake at dusk, or have Henry, the lodge chef, pack another picnic basket.

A picnic. Filomena smiled to herself. It was the perfect answer. She owed him a picnic, she decided. After all, he'd once invited her on one. But this time she wouldn't let the conversation degenerate into business subjects the way it had last time. With her mind made up, she headed for the lodge kitchen. Henry always had plenty of picnic food available. She would pick her favorite items and pinch a bottle of fumé blanc from the cellar. Her father wouldn't care.

Half an hour later, basket slung on her arm, she went in search of Trent. She found him reading a book on the patio overlooking the lake. He looked up as she strode toward him. His eyes moved over her appreciatively, taking in the yellow band holding back her red mane, and yellow tie-front shirt that exposed her flat midriff and the white, hip-riding pants that lovingly shaped her thighs and tapered narrowly down to her ankles. Filomena saw the sensual awareness in his gaze just before he masked it with an expression of polite interest.

"Going somewhere?" he asked casually, closing the book.

"Uh-huh. Want to come along?" She realized this was the first time she had ever invited him anywhere, and for some reason she felt vaguely nervous.

"That depends," he said teasingly.

"On what?" She kept her smile bright and breezy, but she still wasn't sure of what would happen next.

"On what you've got in the basket," Trent explained, folding his hands behind his head as he watched her from the depths of the lounger.

"A bottle of Dad's best fumé blanc, chicken salad sandwiches, a huge bag of potato chips and two slices of chocolate cake."

Trent came out of the chair at once. "Hell, why didn't you say so right off? Let's go."

"My mother always did say that the way to a man's heart was through his stomach. But I never really believed her. I always gave men credit for being a little smarter than that."

"You should listen to your mother more." Trent draped an arm around her shoulders. "Where are we going to eat this feast?"

Filomena hesitated and glanced up at him out of the corner of her eye. "I was thinking about going back to the place where we had the last picnic."

"Lead on."

Filomena's smile became a shade more brilliant. This wasn't going to be so hard, after all. All she had to do was get Trent alone somewhere, feed him some good food and wine and he was sure to take matters into his own hands, just as he had in Portland.

Unfortunately things didn't go quite as smoothly as she had planned. They found the isolated picnic spot, spread out the blanket Filomena had packed in the basket and munched their way through the food and wine. But matters ground to a halt right there. Trent showed no interest in taking over the seduction.

This was ridiculous, Filomena thought as she ate the last pickle and wondered frantically how to extend the picnic now that the food was gone. They had talked about everything from business to fishing, but they hadn't touched on the subject of Filomena Cromwell and Trent Ravinder. Filomena got the impression that if she wanted the subject brought up, she was going to have to do it herself.

It surprised and annoyed her to discover that she had such an aversion to risking rejection. She had never thought of herself as a coward before. But, then, she had never pursued a man since that awful year with Brady Paxton. It was easier and safer to let the men do the running. Unfortunately, although he'd gotten off to a flying start, Trent seemed to have slowed down considerably.

"I'd like to pick up a case of that wine when I return to Portland," Trent said conversationally as he packed the empty bottle back into the basket. "Your dad has excellent taste."

"Yes," Filomena agreed, propping herself on one elbow while she watched him replace the rest of the picnic things. "He likes everything first class at the lodge."

"It shows. He's a good businessman."

"I know." Filomena frowned. "Trent?"

"Hmm?"

"Did you want to rush back to the lodge right away?"

"Not particularly." He looked at her.

"Good." She smiled. "I was thinking we could stay here a while. There's plenty of privacy, and no one's expecting us or anything."

"I know. I should have brought my book along. Great place to sit and read. Maybe I'll take a nap instead."

"Oh." Filomena was slightly disconcerted. She hadn't been expecting that. "You don't look tired."

"I'm not, but I'm on vacation. I'm supposed to do things like take naps and read in the shade after a picnic," he explained with a smile as he settled down with his back braced against the tree. He looked out over the lake. "This is a beautiful place, isn't it?"

"Having grown up here, I guess I take it for granted," she admitted absently. "Trent?"

"Hmm?" He was watching the sunlight on the water, apparently mesmerized by it.

"I was thinking about . . . about us."

"Were you?"

"And about the other night in Portland," she went on with dogged determination. "It was special, wasn't it?" She held her breath.

"Yes," he said quietly, "it was."

She began to breathe again. "I'm glad you think so. I mean, I was beginning to wonder if . . ."

"If what, Filomena?"

She studied his profile, unable to tell what he was thinking. "Nothing. It's just that you haven't said much about it since we got back."

"Neither have you," he pointed out.

She winced. That was true. Changing position on the blanket, she edged her way closer to where he was sitting. One leg was drawn up in front of him, and he had his arm across his knee. His attention was still on the sunlight dancing on the lake. "Well, I'm bringing the subject up now," she told him with a touch of aggression.

"So you are." He didn't move. "What exactly did you want to discuss?"

Filomena felt her patience snap. She sat up and leaned toward him, her brows coming together in a fierce line across her nose. "I don't exactly want to discuss anything at all!"

He gave her a politely inquiring glance. "Then why bring up the subject in the first place?"

"I thought it might be a good excuse to kiss you," she declared rashly and threw herself into his arms. Automatically he caught her, cradling her across his thighs. "You haven't done any more than give me a couple of good-night pecks on the cheek since we got back from Portland." She put her arms around his neck and pulled his head down to hers. She kissed him with all the passion and need she'd discovered that night in Portland and which she'd been bottling up inside herself ever since.

Trent didn't even try to resist. His mouth parted under the pressure of her lips, and he willingly returned the hungry embrace. When Filomena realized that his desire was as strong as it had ever been, she breathed a sigh of relief and nestled closer. Her hand rested possessively on the front of his shirt.

When she broke the kiss at last, she was breathless and flushed. Her eyes sparkled as she looked up at him. "Why?" she demanded.

He smiled. "Why what?"

"Why haven't you kissed me like that since we got back from Portland?"

His big hand slowly stroked her breast. "I wanted you to realize just how much you trust me."

"What's that supposed to mean?"

He caught a strand of her hair and wrapped it around his finger. "You needed to prove to yourself that you don't have to be afraid of rejection. Not with me."

Filomena stiffened in his arms. "I'm not sure I like being manipulated like that."

His face gentled. "There was more to it than just forcing you to take the chance of making the first move."

"What else was there?" she asked suspiciously.

"Has it occurred to you that I might have wanted a little reassurance that you hadn't forgotten what happened in Portland, either?"

Instantly Filomena was contrite. A warm rush of feeling welled up in her. "Trent, I'm so sorry. I didn't think of it that way."

"I know. You're used to being the one who hovers just out of reach. But sometimes a man likes to know he's wanted, too."

Her eyes were luminous. "I want you, Trent."

"I know, sweetheart. You're convincing me." He lowered his head to hers, and this time the kiss was a sweet mingling of desire and trust.

When Trent's hands went to the knot of Filomena's shirt, she tightened her arms around his neck and whispered shyly to him of her eagerness for his lovemaking.

"Sweetheart, you don't know what you do to me," he accused with a thick groan as he carefully settled her on the blanket and came down beside her.

Her fingers trailed teasingly down the front of his shirt to his waist. Then she let her palms wander lower, seeking the hard evidence of his desire. "I'm learning," she said softly. She undid the buckle of his belt.

THEY DIDN'T GET BACK to the lodge until nearly three-thirty. Hand in hand, Filomena and Trent strolled past the front desk in the main lobby. Meg Cromwell glanced up from some work she was doing behind the counter and smiled fondly.

"There you are, Fil. I was wondering where you'd gone. Don't forget the cocktail party for Shari and Jim tonight. By the way, there was a call for you an hour ago."

"Really? Who?"

"Glenna Sterling."

Filomena's eyes widened. "The bank. She must have heard from the bank." She dropped Trent's hand and grabbed the phone, dialing rapidly.

The instant Glenna came on the line, Filomena knew the news was not good. Her heart sank.

"No luck, Fil. They said we're expanding too fast. They suggested we reapply when we've got a broader distribution base."

"But we need the capital to extend the distribution base in order to broaden it in the first place," Filomena snapped. "That's the whole point." She caught Trent's thoughtful gaze on her.

"I know, Fil. And I had so many ideas for the new line. Look, we knew this was a possibility. We'll just have to start over at another bank. Maybe one that's got a better reputation for loaning money to women entrepreneurs. I'll do some research on that end of things while you're on vacation."

"Maybe I should come back," Filomena said uneasily.

"What's the point? It will take me a while to check out other bank possibilities. You can't accomplish anything here by coming back early. Enjoy your sister's wedding, and I'll see you at the end of the month. This is only a setback, Fil. We've battled through worse."

"True." Filomena hung up the phone and leaned dejectedly back against the counter. She folded her arms across her chest and moodily regarded the tip of her sandal.

"The loan fell through?" Trent asked gently.

"They turned us down cold."

"Maybe now's the time to get hold of a good financial consultant," Trent suggested.

"Maybe. What I'd really like to get hold of is that loan officer's neck. We were counting on that money."

"Never count your chickens before they're hatched, Fil," Meg said with that bracing quality all mothers seem to have in times of trial.

Filomena smiled wryly. "Yes, Mother."

Trent chuckled at her expression and put his arm around her shoulders to lead her toward the patio. "Listen to your mother, Filomena. Better yet, listen to me."

She eyed him warily. "What's your advice?"

"Never count your chickens before they're hatched."

7

"WHAT DO YOU THINK of this, Shari?" Filomena spun around in a neat pirouette, showing off the sleek, bare, body-hugging white knit dress she had chosen for the cocktail party that evening.

Shari, dressed in a demure red silk dress that highlighted her shining blond hair, leaned in the doorway and stared in mingled admiration and astonishment.

The white dress left very little of Filomena to the imagination. The front plunged nearly to the navel, and the back dipped almost to the waist. The skirt was short, exposing a considerable amount of leg, which Filomena had emphasized with a pair of impossibly high heels. There was an innocent gold necklace around the throat, which somehow only served to heighten the outrageousness of the rest of the dress.

"Every time you dress for a party around here, the outfit gets wilder and wilder. There was that little blue number with the tight bodice you wore for the replay of the prom party that exposed half your bosom. The splashy little red-and-yellow number you wore to my 'farewell to singlehood' party raised even the caterer's eyebrows. And then there was the green jersey, which, as Aunt Agnes observed, exposed half your backside. Now this. What are you trying to do? Prepare us for a bridesmaid dress made out of clear plastic food wrap? I'm traumatized at the thought of what you're actually going to wear to my wedding."

Filomena made a face at her sister. "Don't be a prude, Shari. You may have decided to come back to live in Gallant Lake, but your tastes are no more small-town than mine are these days. This dress is considered very hot this season."

"It shows an awful lot of skin, Fil," Shari said dubiously. "It's cute on you, I'll grant you that, but I'm not sure it's right for a Gallant Lake cocktail party. That green jersey thing was about as much as this town can take in the way of high style."

"Nonsense." Filomena paused in front of the mirror to check her hair. She had caught it up in a deceptively casual little twist on the top of her head. Several curling red tendrils trailed down her throat. "I'm sure Gallant Lake society will be able to handle the impact."

"What about Trent?"

"Hmm?" Filomena clipped on dangling, glittery earrings. "What about him?"

"Is he going to be able to handle the impact?"

Filomena frowned at her sister in the mirror. "You don't think he'll like the dress?"

"I think that man is rapidly developing a streak of possessiveness where you're concerned. I'm not so sure he's going to want Brady Paxton and everyone else ogling you tonight."

Filomena paused in the act of applying her lipstick. "I haven't made a habit of letting any man tell me what I can and can't wear for the past nine years, Shari. I'm not about to start now. Besides, Trent isn't a small-town type, either. He isn't going to be upset about this dress."

Shari smiled knowingly. "We'll see."

Filomena narrowed her eyes. "What could he do except mumble about it, anyway?" she asked, remembering his grumbling remarks about the green jersey she had worn to the country club.

"Put his foot down?" Shari suggested helpfully.

Filomena giggled. "Not likely. What good would it do him? He's smart enough not to try anything like that."

"If you say so." Shari looked her sister over again. "It is a darling dress on you, even if it does cover less than a swimsuit. Gallant Lake won't forget it soon, that's for sure. Enjoying your vacation, Fil?"

Filomena met her sister's perceptive gaze. "I was enjoying it a lot more before I heard the bad news from Glenna this afternoon."

"Mom told me," Shari said sympathetically. "But she said Trent hinted at being able to get you and Glenna some professional advice from a hotshot financial consultant?"

"That's what he said. He thinks it might be helpful. He says Glenna and I are at a very precarious point in our business. We've got to make some decisions and plans instead of just growing willy-nilly as fast as we can."

"Mom and Dad are extremely pleased with themselves, you know."

"Because they sicced Trent on to me and things seem to be working out?"

"Uh-huh."

"Well, what can I say?" Filomena asked with a grin. "They deserve to take some credit."

"Mom says Trent has the same look in his eyes as Jim did when he first started dating me. Lean and hungry."

Filomena dabbed on some perfume and headed for the door. She looked at her sister. "Lean and hungry, huh? Well, what do you say we go downstairs and confront the lions?"

Shari laughed. "You go first. I want to watch Trent's face when he sees that dress."

Filomena shrugged and walked toward the staircase. She was looking forward to the evening. It was the first time she had been òut with Trent on anything resembling a real date since they had returned from Portland.

Trent was standing in the hall along with her parents and Jim Devore. He looked up from something he was saying to Amery and saw Filomena as she flitted lightly down the stairs. She smiled happily at him, aware that her parents and Jim were all staring at the white dress.

Trent was the only one who didn't appear shocked. His jade eyes moved over the dress with cool deliberation and then went back to Filomena's face. He didn't say a word.

"Fil, dear," Meg Cromwell began in a worried tone, "isn't that dress a bit . . . a bit . . ." Her voice trailed off.

"I warned her," Shari said blithely as she stepped forward to accept Jim's kiss. "But she thinks Gallant Lake can handle it."

Jim grinned at Trent. "The question is, can Trent handle it? Good luck, pal. I warned you about the perils of trying to manage a female from this household."

"I see your point," Trent murmured, his eyes still on Filomena, who was smiling far too sweetly.

Amery Cromwell cleared his throat and made a production out of looking at his watch. "Uh, maybe we'd better be on our way, Meg. Shari's going to go with Jim, and Trent says he'll bring Filomena in his own car." He took his wife's arm and started determinedly toward the door. Meg glanced back doubtfully at Filomena and allowed herself to be led out of sight.

"We'd better be going, too, love," Jim said smoothly, reaching for Shari's hand. "I have a weak stomach. Can't stand the sight of blood."

"You're a doctor!" Shari reminded him as he hurried her outside.

"That's why I know I can't stand the sight of blood." Jim shut the door, leaving Filomena and Trent in the hall.

Filomena stood on the bottom step and looked at Trent expectantly. "Well? Shall we be on our way? Let's take my car."

He walked forward slowly, something between amusement and determination showing in his eyes. His mouth edged upward in a faint smile. "You couldn't resist, could you?"

"Resist what?" she asked innocently.

"Filomena, my sweet, I think you have developed a nasty habit of equating large size with stupidity. Just because I seem larger than the average dinosaur to you, it doesn't automatically follow that I have the brain of one."

She laughed at him with her eyes, enjoying the fact that because she was standing on the bottom step and had on a pair of high heels she was actually looking down on him. "Are you trying to tell me you're smarter than the average dinosaur?"

"I'd like to think so. But even if I'm not, I still have size on my side. Go and change the dress, sweetheart," he ordered gently.

Filomena blinked. "You don't like the dress?"

"The dress," he said evenly, "is designed to make a man want to pick you up and carry you off to bed. Unfortunately we are going to a cocktail party, not bed."

She reached out and patted him on the head, smiling with womanly assurance. "So that's the trouble. Shari was right. You're feeling a little possessive. Well, don't worry about a thing, Trent. This is very definitely a look-but-don't-touch sort of dress. No one at the cocktail party is going to pick me up and haul me off to bed." She paused, grinning wickedly. "Unless, of course, you get carried away and do something rash."

He ignored the reassuring pat on the head. His faint smile didn't waver. "Shari was wrong. I am not feeling a little possessive. I am feeling very possessive. You've teased and tormented Gallant Lake often enough since you've been here. You don't need to consolidate your victory tonight. Run along and change, honey. It's getting late."

Filomena studied his expression and came to the conclusion that beneath the slight smile and the flicker of amusement in his eyes, Trent was serious. She drew a deep breath and let it out slowly. "Why do I get the feeling this is a turning point in our relationship?"

"It's not a turning point in our relationship. It's a turning point for you. You've had your fun with the good folks of Gallant Lake. Change the dress, Filomena."

She drummed her fingers on the banister. "Or what?"

"Or I'll use my size and small brain power to help you change it."

Filomena smiled grimly. "Threats, Trent?"

"Promises, sweetheart."

There was a long pause. The hall clock ticked loudly in the silence as Filomena assessed Trent's mood and determination.

"Let's consider this from a mature, rational viewpoint, Trent," she finally said carefully. "There are several potential problems here. If I allow you to intimidate me into changing my clothes, my entire family will know I am basically a female wimp as soon as I walk into the party."

"If you don't change your clothes, your entire family will be forced to the conclusion that I'm the wimp," Trent pointed out blandly.

Harlequin's

Best-Ever "Get Acquainted" Offer

Look what we'd give to hear from you

6 FREE GIFTS 6

Return This Sticker
and Get 6 Gifts—FREE
Compliments of Harlequin

**GET ALL YOU ARE
ENTITLED TO—AFFIX STICKER
TO RETURN CARD—MAIL TODAY**

This is our most fabulous offer ever...
AND THERE'S STILL MORE INSIDE.
Let's get acquainted.
Let's become friends—

Look what we've got for you:

...A FREE compact Harlequin umbrella
...plus a sampler set of 4 terrific
Harlequin Temptation novels, specially
selected by our editors.

...PLUS a surprise mystery gift
that will delight you.

All this just for trying our Reader Service!

With your trial, you'll get SNEAK PREVIEWS
to 4 new Harlequin Temptation novels a month—
before they're available in stores—with 10% off
retail on any books you keep (just $2.24 each)—
and FREE home delivery besides.

Plus There's More!

You'll also get our newsletter, packed with news of your favorite authors and upcoming books—FREE! And as a valued reader, we'll be sending you additional free gifts from time to time—as a token of our appreciation.

THERE IS NO CATCH. You're not required to buy a single book, ever. You may cancel Reader Service privileges anytime, if you want. The free gifts are yours anyway. It's a super sweet deal if ever there was one. Try us and see!

Get 4 FREE full-length Harlequin Temptation novels.

Plus

this handy compact umbrella

Plus

a surprise free gift

▼ PLUS LOTS MORE! MAIL THIS CARD TODAY ▼

Harlequin's Best-Ever "Get Acquainted" Offer

Yes, I'll try the Harlequin Reader Service under the terms outlined on the opposite page. Send me 4 free Harlequin Temptation novels, a free compact umbrella and a free mystery gift.

142 CIX MDMX

PLACE STICKER FOR 6 FREE GIFTS HERE

NAME

ADDRESS _____ APT. _____

CITY

STATE _____ ZIP CODE _____

Don't forget...

…Return this card today to receive your 4 free books, free compact umbrella and free mystery gift.

…You will receive books before they're available in stores and at a discount off retail prices.

…No obligation. Keep only the books you want, cancel anytime.

If offer card is missing, write to: Harlequin Reader Service, 901 Fuhrmann Blvd., P.O. Box 1394, Buffalo, NY 14240-1394.

"Not likely," she said, airily dismissing his claim. "No one would ever think of you as a wimp. Another problem with me changing my dress is that you might be left with the impression that you can order me around whenever the mood takes you. It's an attitude a lot of large people have toward those who are shorter and smaller. It's one of the fundamental reasons, I think, why men in general have always assumed they have the right to dominate women. The world would be a much different place if women were taller and stronger than men. All the attitudes between the sexes would be reversed."

Trent glanced at the stainless-steel watch on his wrist. "I'm not sure we have time for anthropological speculation."

But Filomena was warming to her subject now. "Just think how different everything would be, Trent. If women were taller and bigger and stronger, they would be the ones who made the decisions and gave the orders. They would be the ones who felt possessive and protective and dominant."

"I think we're wandering from the main point here."

She waved that aside, her eyes lighting with enthusiasm for her new subject. "Everyone would assume it was natural for men to stay home and take care of the children and dress in frilly little dresses. After all, they would be the weaker sex, right? Our whole family structure would be different. What's more, women wouldn't be victimized so much. They wouldn't have to walk around in fear of rape or domestic violence. They wouldn't have to pretend they weren't as bright as men. They wouldn't have to play games—"

"Filomena," Trent broke in with the first hint of diminishing patience, "I have the distinct impression you are trying to play games with me right now and I think

I'd better warn you I am not in the mood. Go and change the dress."

"Why should I?" she challenged. "Give me one good reason why I shouldn't wear exactly what I want to wear tonight!"

Trent shoved back the edges of his light-colored linen jacket and planted his hands on his hips. His eyes narrowed coolly, and the last of the indulgent smile faded from his mouth. He looked up at Filomena. "You want one good reason? I'll give you one good reason. We are not living in your dreamworld. We are living in a world where you happen to be a lot smaller than I am. *Go upstairs and change the dress.*"

Filomena stood still for an instant longer. Trent's voice hadn't risen, but, then, he didn't have to raise it in order to make his point.

"Might does not make right," she proclaimed.

"No, but it has a hell of an influence on the final outcome, doesn't it?"

Filomena knew when she was beaten. She lifted her chin and gave him a disdainful smile. "Just remember what happened to the dinosaurs." She swung around and walked back up the stairs as Trent's laughter filled the hall.

When she reached her bedroom, she caught sight of herself in the mirror and smiled suddenly. The white dress did, indeed, expose a great deal of skin. Shocking Gallant Lake no longer mattered. What mattered was that Trent was showing every sign of being possessive and jealous. The man was falling in love with her, she thought happily. Given that delightful assurance, she was in the mood to make a few concessions.

Ten minutes later she came back down the stairs wearing a close-fitting, off-the-shoulder dress fashioned in warm peach tones. There was a flounce at the knee to give the dress some sophisticated playfulness, but there was nothing in the design that could give Trent anything to complain about. She paused once more on the bottom step.

"Satisfied?" she asked with a haughty smile.

He grinned. "It'll do." He reached for her hand. "Thank you, Filomena."

"For what?"

"For not making me look like a wimpy dinosaur in front of your family."

She slanted him a sardonic glance. "You owe me one."

He laughed as he opened the front door and shut it behind them. "Trust you to find a way to salvage something from the situation. Okay, I owe you one." He paused on the front step, leaned down and brushed his mouth lingeringly against hers. "When are you going to collect?" he murmured.

"Probably when you least expect it." She started down the path to where the cars were parked. "Let's take the Porsche."

"There's no need. I think everyone in Gallant Lake has already seen it."

"That's not why I want to take it," she explained, digging her keys out of her purse. "I want to take it so that I can do the driving."

Trent groaned as he reluctantly slid into the passenger seat beside her. "Is this going to be my punishment for having won the battle over the dress?"

"You sound nervous," she taunted as she turned the key in the ignition and slipped the car into gear.

"You drive like a bat out of hell. Naturally I'm nervous."

"I," declared Filomena as gravel hissed under the wheels, "am an excellent driver." The Porsche shot out of the parking area like a Thoroughbred out of a racing gate. By the time the vehicle hit the main road around the lake, it was moving at a very brisk clip. Filomena drove with both hands on the wheel and a great deal of attention. She loved the feel of the car as it responded to her lightest touch. Deliberately she put it through its paces on the curves.

Trent endured the situation in absolute silence for nearly ten minutes and then he said quietly, "All right, that's enough."

"Enough what?" she asked politely.

"You've gotten even for the battle over the dress. Now slow down and show some common sense."

There was an edge to his voice that hadn't been present when he'd ordered her to change her clothes. Filomena realized Trent had had enough of the Porsche's gymnastics. Obediently she slowed the car to a more sedate pace. There was a long silence.

"I'm not used to it, you know," she finally said.

"Not used to having to adjust your life to accommodate a man? I know. It works both ways. I'm not accustomed to feeling this possessive about a woman. But I think we'll both learn to handle it."

There was another long silence, this time a thoughtful one that lasted until Filomena parked the Porsche in the driveway of the Aikens's lakeside home. She turned off the ignition and sat quietly surveying the cars that were parked up and down the street.

"Just remember you still owe me a favor."

"I'll remember," he said.

Filomena was quiet for another moment. "It looks like the Aikens have invited everyone in Gallant Lake tonight."

Trent opened his door and got out. "Don't worry, that dress is going to make an even bigger impression than the white one would have."

She looked down at the peach-colored dress and grimaced as she climbed out of the car. "Why do you say that?"

He grinned at her in the street light. "Just a guess, but I have a hunch most of your old high school girlfriends have been hearing about your clothes for days. They've probably all gone out and bought themselves the most outrageous outfits they could find in an effort to compete tonight. When you show up in something respectable and modest, they're all going to feel terribly overdressed."

Filomena burst out laughing. "Since when did you become such an expert on the female psyche?"

"I'm a fast learner." He took her arm and led her toward the open doors of the house.

It didn't take Filomena long to decide she had been right when she guessed that just about everyone in town had been invited to the Aikens's party. The crowd filled the living room, den and kitchen and spilled out onto the patio. There was food everywhere, and Todd Aiken had set up a generous bar near the door. Few people noticed the new arrivals at first. In the crush it was difficult to see who was coming and going.

"I'll get us a drink," Trent said. "Don't move."

Filomena nodded, watching him head for the bar. His height made it easy to keep track of him in the crowd.

"Fil! There you are. What in the world took you and Trent so long to get here? I was just about to phone home and see what was going on." Shari emerged from the throng, smiling down at her sister. Her eyes went over the demure peach-colored outfit. "Aha. I was right. He made you change your dress."

"Trent did not *make* me change my dress," Filomena informed her. "We had a discussion on the subject, and after some rational arguments on both sides, I decided not to make him look like a wimp."

Shari gave a shout of laughter that caused several nearby heads to turn. "As if you could." At that moment Trent appeared with a glass of wine for Filomena and a mug of beer for himself.

"Hello, Shari," he said easily. "Where's Jim?"

"Talking about the merits of flu shots with the mother of one of his patients. I was just asking Filomena what took you both so long to get here and then I realized she had on a different dress."

Filomena had had enough. "If anyone says one more word about the fact that I changed clothes this evening, I swear I will strip naked right here in the Aikens's living room and give you all something to really talk about. Do I make myself clear?"

"Don't say another word, Shari," Trent advised. "I, for one, believe her."

"Oh, so do I," Shari said quickly. "You can only push Fil so far and then she goes up in flames."

Another voice interrupted before anyone could comment on that. An attractive dark-haired woman of Filomena's age and height pushed her way through the crowd. "Fil! There you are. I heard you were going to be here tonight. Long time, no see. Geez, you look good. Just like everyone says."

"Hi, Liz. I almost didn't recognize you." Filomena laughed at her old acquaintance. "You're looking very good yourself." She hadn't seen Liz Sawyer since high school. Liz had been two years ahead of her. She was about Filomena's height.

"I'll bet you recognized the dress, though, didn't you?" Liz spun around, displaying the brightly patterned knit sweater and silk skirt she was wearing. "It's a Cromwell & Sterling, naturally. I love it. My wardrobe is filled with your things. They fit so beautifully."

Pleased, Filomena thanked her and made introductions. It wasn't long before a lively group of young women had formed, and Filomena became involved in a discussion of her travels in Tahiti and India in search of patterns and exotic materials. She looked up briefly when Trent touched her arm and said he was going to find her father.

"Okay," she said with a smile. "I'll see you later."

He kissed her forehead with casual possessiveness and walked away in search of his fishing buddy. Liz and the others stared after him with speculative expressions, then they turned back to Filomena and demanded to know what the fashion forecasts were for the coming season.

After a while it dawned on Filomena that she was enjoying herself. For the first time since she had returned to Gallant Lake she wasn't thinking about causing a sensation or making certain everyone knew just how different life was for her now. Instead, she relaxed and renewed old acquaintances.

Life in Gallant Lake in her younger days hadn't been all that bad, she thought. There had been a lot of young women besides herself who hadn't made the cheerleading squad or who had lacked a date for the homecoming dance. Most of them had survived quite well, just as she had.

When the cigarette smoke and the heat became a little overwhelming, Filomena excused herself to get another glass of cool wine. She spoke to her host for a few minutes as he wielded bottles behind the small bar and then she decided to get a breath of fresh air out on the terrace.

She glanced around to see if she could spot Trent before she went outside and saw him standing across the room talking with her father and two other men. From their serious expressions, Filomena assumed they were either discussing the possibilities for a third world war or the merits of certain fishing locations on the lake. Men sometimes lacked a sense of proportion about life, she thought with an inner smile.

A balmy breeze greeted her as she walked through the open sliding glass doors. She was pleased to see she had the terrace to herself, at least for a while. She needed a few minutes to recover from the cheerful noise and confusion inside. Glass in hand, she moved to the far side of the terrace and leaned against the rail to contemplate the moonlit lake.

It was the first time all evening that she'd had a few minutes to herself. She used them to think about Trent Ravinder.

She wouldn't have changed that white dress for any other man on the face of the earth. It was a sobering thought. Strange how the little things sometimes held so much importance and meaning.

"Fil?"

Brady Paxton's voice interrupted her reflections.

"Hello, Brady," Filomena said without much enthusiasm. She didn't bother to turn around. Instead, she continued to lean on the railing, her drink cradled loosely in one hand.

"I've been looking for you," he said earnestly, moving toward her. "We need to talk."

"I don't think so, Brady."

He came to a halt beside her and joined her in leaning on the railing. The breeze ruffled his tawny hair and brought the scent of his cologne to Filomena's nostrils. She wrinkled her nose and decided she didn't like the fragrance.

Brady let out a long sigh. "All right, I was a little slow in the beginning, but I've got it figured out now. You're really slick, Fil. I'll give you that. I never would have believed you could pull it off."

Filomena tapped one long nail on the cedar railing. "Pull what off, Brady?"

"No wonder you didn't want to do a deal with me when I offered you a commission the other day. You had your own plans, didn't you? You must have laughed all the way home about my offer of a five percent commission."

"Not exactly," she said dryly, wondering where this was going. "How's your wife? Is she here tonight? Maybe she'd like to join us."

"Forget Gloria," Brady snapped. "We're talking business, you and I."

"I'm not talking business. I'm out here to get some fresh air."

"You are one tough lady these days, aren't you, Fil? Who'd have thought you, of all people, would turn out like this? You were so sweet nine years ago."

"You mean I was so stupid nine years ago. I actually trusted you, Brady. Talk about dumb. Ah, well, it takes some of us longer to grow up than it does others, I guess. But I did eventually grow up."

He looked down at her with hot, intent eyes. "You haven't forgotten, have you? You still want me. I can tell. Beneath all that bravado, you still want me."

A slow, mocking smile shaped her mouth as she turned to him. "If you think that, you're a bigger fool now than I was at nineteen. I wouldn't have you if you came served on a silver platter."

His mood shifted abruptly. Anger appeared in his eyes and in the twist of his mouth. "Because you think you can do better, is that it? You think now that you've got your hooks into Ravinder, you've got it made? Think again, lady. He's big time. You're nothing more than a summer fling to him. If you've got any sense you know that and you'll use it to get the information we both want. But you won't fool yourself into believing he's serious about you."

"The way I once fooled myself into thinking you were serious about me?" she asked with a dangerous lightness.

Even in the shadows, the flush was evident on Brady's cheeks. His gaze grew more intense. "Nine years ago I had to make a decision. If it's any consolation to you, I've paid for that decision. I am not a happily married man, Fil. There have been a lot of nights when I've lain awake wondering what would have happened if you and I had stayed together. The only reason I haven't divorced Gloria is because her father would dissolve the insurance partnership."

"How about the fact that you've got two children? Isn't that a factor in your decision not to get a divorce? Or don't they count, Brady? You don't have any qualms about hurting people, do you? But heaven forbid you should jeopardize a business arrangement. Well, you made the right decision nine years ago. I am very, very glad you didn't marry me. Your wife and children have my deepest sympathy."

"Don't give me that garbage, Fil," he said hoarsely. "You don't feel sorry for them or anyone else because you're too busy looking out for number one these days. I've figured out what you're up to, you know. You don't fool me."

"Is that right?" she taunted. "Just what am I up to?"

"You're having an affair with Ravinder. The whole town knows it."

"No kidding?"

"We all know you went to Portland with him for the night a few days ago. Hell, Gloria practically hit me over the head with the news when I got home from work that day. She couldn't wait to tell me. Wanted me to know what a little tramp you are and how you weren't exactly hanging around Gallant Lake to seduce me. She said you had bigger fish to fry. That's when I realized what you were up to."

"I think it would be best if you didn't say anything more, Brady."

He ignored that. "You think you know what you're doing, but you're going to land in real trouble if you don't listen to me. I know you've started the affair with Ravinder in order to find out what Asgard's intentions are. But you can't do a thing with the information unless you deal with me. I have options on just about every decent piece of land on the lake. Sooner or later you're going to have to work with me. Now, I'm willing to raise your commission a bit."

"Forget it, Brady."

"All right, we can form a partnership, if that's what you want."

"I said forget it, Brady."

He was infuriated by her quiet refusal. "Who do you think you're going to sell the information to, if not to me? You don't have any choice, damn it!"

Filomena finally lost what remained of her patience. She whirled around to confront him face-to-face. "Brady Paxton, you are a fool, even if you do own most of the good land around Gallant Lake. Number one, Asgard is not interested in putting in a resort development around here. Number two, even if the company was interested and even if I knew which tracts of land it wanted to buy, I wouldn't tell you, no matter how much money you offered for the information. Want to know why?"

"Because you think Ravinder's in love with you? Is that it?"

"Because I know I am in love with him," Filomena corrected bluntly. "And what's more I'm going to marry him. If you think I'd betray the man I'm going to marry for the sake of a lousy real estate deal, then I think it's safe to say you never did know me very well. Now why don't you trot back inside and find your wife. I'm sure she's looking for you."

"Why, you little bitch!"

Brady's hand came up as he loomed over Filomena. She held her ground, the wineglass clenched in her hand in case she had to hurl it in self-defense. But the confrontation never got a chance to explode into violence. Trent spoke from the doorway, his voice slicing like cold fire through the shadows.

"If you so much as touch her, Paxton, I'll take you apart so thoroughly they won't ever get all the pieces back together again."

8

FILOMENA WHIRLED AROUND and saw Trent striding swiftly across the terrace. With a little gasp of relief, she set her glass down on the railing and ran forward to throw herself against his chest. His right arm went out to grasp her and hold her close. She was swallowed up immediately in the confines of his embrace. He felt very large and sturdy and safe, she reflected. There were times when size was comforting.

"I'm sorry about this," she mumbled into his jacket.

He crushed her gently. "I'm not." Then he raised his voice slightly. "I think you'd better go back inside, Paxton. There's no point in pestering my fiancée anymore. She wouldn't sell you the information you want, even if she had it, which she doesn't. And by now you've probably figured out for yourself she has no intention of letting herself get dragged into an affair with you. But if you can't grasp that simple concept, then take my word for it that if you come near her again, I'll slaughter you. Do we have an understanding?"

Brady edged around him, his face set in bitter, resentful lines as he started back toward the sliding glass doors. "She's playing games, Ravinder. If you're as smart as people seem to think, you won't be fooled by them. I'll admit she's turned into a hot little piece of tail, but she's definitely got her eye on the main chance. She's a real businesswoman these days. Better keep that in mind if you know what's good—"

Brady never finished the sentence. Filomena felt Trent's body tighten briefly and then uncoil with the speed and power of a natural predator. She barely had time to realize she was free from his comforting grasp when she heard the ominous thud and the sound of air whooshing from Brady's chest.

"Oh, my God," she breathed, shocked by the swiftness with which it had all happened as much as by the violence itself. She found herself staring down at Brady's crumpled body. He raised himself on one elbow, gasping for air and glared at Trent who was standing over him.

"*Now* do we understand each other?" Trent asked.

"You bastard, you're welcome to her!" Brady scrambled to his feet, brushed furiously at his clothing and stalked painfully back into the house.

"What if he sues?" Filomena asked faintly, voicing the first fear that came to mind.

"Trust me, he won't." Trent looked at her and shook his head slightly when he saw the anxious expression on her face. "He won't want to have to explain how it happened," he elaborated. "Too embarrassing."

"Oh." Filomena chewed on her lower lip, considering that. "It would be, wouldn't it? Brady would hate to humiliate himself like that."

"Yes."

She eyed him with a sense of trepidation. "Well, don't keep me in suspense. How much did you hear?"

There was a short pause. "Enough. But the only part that mattered was the bit about marrying me."

"I was afraid of that." Filomena sighed and went to lean against the railing again. "I'm sorry, Trent. It just sort of slipped out. I wasn't thinking, really. I wanted to convince Brady I had absolutely no interest in him, and he said something about having an affair with you and I just sort of took it from there." She picked up her wineglass and took a shaky sip for courage. "Sometimes I do things on impulse. An old habit."

"I know the feeling." Absently he rubbed his knuckles as he moved toward her. His eyes were very brilliant in the moonlight. "Occasionally I do a few things on impulse, too. But that doesn't mean I always regret them. How about you?"

Her fingers tightened on the glass in her hand as she looked up at him with a clear, honest longing in her eyes. "I don't usually regret the things I do on impulse, either. I figure that . . . that fundamentally they're really not all that impulsive. Sometimes they're just things my subconscious has been mulling over for a while, and suddenly the truth jumps out without any warning."

Trent's eyes softened but lost none of their brilliance. He lifted a hand and stroked the side of her cheek. "Tell me this great truth that just jumped out at you without any warning," he urged.

"I . . . I just realized as I was talking to Brady that I've fallen in love with you."

Trent buried his lips in her hair. "I can hardly believe it."

"I know I've taken you by surprise," she said hurriedly, "but, you see, I—"

He hushed her with a tender finger on her lips. "It's all right, sweetheart. It's all right. I'm not complaining, believe me. It's just that it all happened so quickly. I think I'm in shock."

"So quickly?"

He smiled. "I fell in love with you within a few hours of meeting you, elf."

"Oh, Trent, really?"

"Really. I've known where I was headed for a long time now, and I told myself I was succeeding in coaxing you along in the same direction. But to be honest, I thought it was going to take you a lot longer to arrive at the same destination. You've been so uninterested in love and marriage that I figured it would take a lot more effort than this on my part to get you to the altar."

She smiled up at him. "Disappointed at an easy victory?"

"Are you kidding? I'm just grateful you came to your senses so quickly. Saves me a lot of work. I'm not about to question my luck."

She wrapped her arms around him with fierce longing. "Oh, Trent, I'm so glad. I can't believe it," she rushed on as happiness overtook her. "I never realized where it was all leading. I must have been blind. My God, I've never felt like this about anyone. Why didn't I understand sooner?"

He laughed softly, his fingers urgent on her skin as he held her close. "You were too busy staying out of my reach while you showed Gallant Lake you've gone big time. You didn't see the tree because you were looking at the whole forest."

She laughed against his shirt. "Such a big tree, too. So you took me to Portland and made sure you got my full attention for a while, is that it?"

"After that, everything fell into place very nicely."

"You're a very clever man," she said.

"I know."

"And modest, too."

"It's tough to be modest when you're this clever, but I try," he agreed modestly.

Her eyes were filled with joy as she raised her head to meet his gaze. "Making me fall in love with you is one thing, but I told Brady that I was going to marry you. That's another matter altogether. Are you clever enough to keep me dangling while you steer clear of marriage?"

"I'm not even going to try to avoid marriage," he told her with rough passion, and then he kissed her thoroughly. When he finally lifted his mouth from hers, she was trembling. He looked down at her with satisfaction and smiled. "You're committed, you know. You've told Brady, and that means everyone at the party will have heard by now."

"A daunting thought."

"Uh-huh. In another few minutes I expect to see your family stampeding out here to demand confirmation."

"You don't look nervous."

"I'm not," he said. "Are you?"

Filomena shook her head with grave certainty. "No," she whispered. "It's what I want. I never would have guessed it, but it's what I want. Trent, there's so much to talk about. So much we have to discuss. I want to know—"

"Filomena! Trent! What the devil is going on?" Amery Cromwell's voice bellowed across the terrace.

Trent turned with Filomena in his arms as Amery led the charge. He was followed by Meg and Shari and a grinning Jim Devore. Uncle George and Aunt Agnes brought up the rear. George was waving a bottle of champagne and calling for glasses. Several other people trickled out onto the terrace behind them, wearing curious expressions.

Trent surveyed the assembled crowd of interested faces. "It's tough to keep things quiet in a small town, isn't it?" he observed.

THE FOLLOWING AFTERNOON Filomena lounged comfortably against Trent who had his back braced against a tree near the water's edge. He had one arm wrapped around her, and with his free hand he was tossing occasional pebbles into the lake.

"Are you sure we know what we're doing?" Filomena asked with lazy amusement.

"Relax. I'll take care of everything."

"Maybe we should have waited until after Shari's wedding to announce our engagement. I don't want to steal any of her thunder. This is her special time."

Trent grinned. "Don't worry about it. Shari was thrilled, just as everyone else in the family was. It might have been tacky to get married ahead of her, but no one's going to hold the engagement announcement against us."

"You're sure?"

"I'm positive. I had a long talk with your father about it," he informed her.

"You *what*?" She pulled away from him to peer up into his face. "What do you mean you had a long talk with him? What sort of long talk? And why wasn't I present?"

"You weren't present because you didn't get up at five-thirty to go fishing with us this morning."

"If I'd known you were going to discuss something important, I might have made the effort," Filomena grumbled.

"It was men's talk," Trent explained condescendingly.

"Is that right? And what precisely got said between you two men?"

"Mostly we talked about how glad everyone is that I'm going to marry you. The rest of the family can stop worrying about you now. You're not getting any younger, you know. It's all well and good to be a successful career woman, but your family is convinced you need a man to love. They appreciate the fact that I've volunteered. I detected more than appreciation, to be honest. I got the feeling that a vast sense of relief was felt by all concerned."

Filomena collapsed in outraged laughter and began pummeling him mercilessly. "Arrogant, overbearing, egotistical male." Her small blows rained over him like popcorn.

He grinned, catching hold of her wrists. "Hey, is that any way to treat the man who is going to be your lord and master?"

"You're really getting into this, aren't you?" she accused with gleaming eyes. "I had no idea you were so eager to become a husband."

His expression sobered. "I had no idea you were so eager to become a wife."

"I wasn't," she admitted, growing more serious. "My life has been full. I thought I had everything I wanted or needed."

"And when you thought of marriage, you thought of walking in on Paxton and Gloria nine years ago," he finished for her.

Filomena nodded. "I suppose so. It wasn't just walking in on them, you understand. That was bad enough. But the whole town found out about it within twenty-four hours. When Brady broke the engagement and announced he was marrying Gloria, I thought I was going to die of humiliation. I wanted to run and hide and never show my face around here again." She paused. "I was very young in many ways."

"That kind of scene would traumatize anyone." Trent tangled his fingers in her hair. "Especially someone like you, sweetheart."

"What do you mean?"

He smiled. "You can put on a good act these days with those showy clothes and that confident chatter, but deep inside you're still soft and innocent in a lot of ways." She started to protest, but he held up his hand. "It's built into you, and you're going to be that way the rest of your life, so don't bother arguing about it."

"How do you know?" she demanded.

"I know every time I take you in my arms."

"I sense a touch of chauvinism here," Filomena said warningly. "Typical of a man to think he knows all there is to know about a woman simply because he's made love to her a few times."

Trent was unfazed. "I don't know all there is to know about you, but I know the important things."

"Such as?"

His eyes softened as he looked down into her face. He touched her breast lightly, cupping it until the nipple stirred eagerly and began to grow taut beneath the fabric of the tropical flower print jumpsuit she was wearing. "I know you've been wary of giving yourself to any man for the past few years, but when you finally gave yourself to me you did it completely. You surrendered totally and honestly. You made me feel more wanted than I've ever felt in my life. You couldn't have done that if you were basically selfish or hard or emotionally brittle."

Filomena drew in her breath, trembling under the warmth of his gaze. "I know a few things about you, too," she managed to say with light challenge.

His mouth crooked. "Is that right?"

She nodded quickly. "You're a good man, an honest man, a man I can trust. I think you're hard in some ways, maybe too rigid about some things, but I expect marriage will soften you up some."

"Think so?"

"Umm." She paused thoughtfully. "The only thing I'm not sure of is why you want to marry me."

He brushed his mouth across her lips. "That's your streak of insecurity showing. Shari was right, you never completely got over what Paxton did to you when you were nineteen. And for the past couple of years you've been running into men who are attracted to Cromwell & Sterling as much as they are to you. No wonder you're a little insecure when it comes to men. But I can fix that."

Filomena rolled her eyes. "For crying out loud. You've been discussing me with my sister, too?"

"I believe in thoroughly researching a project."

"Well, next time you have any questions about me, ask me, understand?"

"Got it."

"All right, tell me why you want to marry me," she persisted.

"You're smart, sexy and lovable. What other reasons do I need?"

"Evelyn Reece said you spent the past year looking for a wife the way you look for choice land for Asgard. She had the impression you had just abandoned the project until you finally ran into me."

Trent's indulgent smile faded, and his eyebrows rose in mild disapproval. "You and Evelyn appear to have had quite a conversation in the ladies' room of that restaurant."

Filomena gave him a complacent look. "Now you know what it's like to be discussed with third parties."

"I'll keep it in mind." It was obvious Trent was not pleased by what Filomena had learned about him behind his back.

"Well?"

"Well, what?" he retorted.

"Have you spent the past year shopping for a wife?"

His displeasure flared in his eyes, but he didn't try to prevaricate. "You want to know what I was doing this past year? All right, I'll tell you. I decided it was time."

"Time to get married? Just like that you decided?" she asked, torn between disbelief and laughter. "I can see it now. The big honcho executive decides he wants to get married, so he sets out to negotiate a wedding the same way he would a land deal. It's wonderful. I love it."

He growled something about her sense of humor and then went doggedly on with his explanation. "I'm thirty-six years old, honey. Until now I've devoted everything to my career. After the disaster of my first marriage, I wasn't all that eager to take the plunge again. I thought there was plenty of time to worry about finding another wife and having a family, but one day I woke up and looked around and realized the important things in life were slipping rapidly out of reach. There wasn't as much time as I had thought. I guess there never is. My career is important to me, but there are other things that are important also. I wanted someone else in my life. I wanted a woman who loved me in my home and in my bed. I wanted a woman to come home to at night, someone to share the highs and the lows with. Does that sound so strange?"

"Nope."

"Then why are you struggling to keep from laughing out loud?" he demanded wryly.

"It's just the thought of you setting out to find a wife in such a methodical fashion." She smiled up at him. "Actually, it's very sweet in a way."

"Sweet, huh?"

"Sweet," she repeated firmly. "Rather touchingly innocent. Go on, tell me what went wrong. Evelyn said you seemed to have abandoned the search."

"When I get back to Portland, I'm going to have a talk with Reece about his wife's tendency to gossip."

"Don't be an idiot," Filomena said fondly. "Evelyn was just being helpful. Now tell me what went wrong during the big search."

Trent shrugged. "I didn't find anyone I wanted to marry. Maybe I was looking too hard. I don't know. Maybe I worried too much about finding someone who wanted me for myself and not my position at Asgard. Whatever the reason, nothing seemed to click. I gave up and went back to my normal routine. Then I decided that what I really needed was a long vacation. I came up here, you arrived at the speed of light in that Porsche and presto, everything fell into place."

He looked so pleased with himself that Filomena began to laugh again. His hand moved on her breast, and her laughter turned into a soft little moan of pleasure. Trent eased her down onto the bed of pine needles.

"Trent?"

"Hmm?" He was busy unbuttoning the front of the jumpsuit.

"When do you want to get married?" Filomena asked hesitantly.

"As soon as possible." He had the top open now and was unbuckling the wide belt. Frowning slightly, he looked down into her face. "Why? Did you want a big wedding like Shari's?"

"No."

"Good. Then there's no reason we can't arrange something small in a few weeks, is there?"

She smiled, shaking her head. "No."

"I think you're going to make me an excellent wife, Filomena Cromwell."

"What makes you say that?"

"You know when to say no and you know when to say yes." He bent to take one budding nipple into his mouth.

Filomena thrust her fingers urgently into his hair, lifting herself into his kiss. "Yes," she whispered in a soft, throaty voice. "Oh, yes, Trent."

He loved the sound of the word "yes" on her lips, Trent decided as he quickly began to lose himself in the warmth and sweetness of Filomena's body. He could never hear it often enough, no matter how long he lived.

A part of him still couldn't believe his good luck. The relationship between himself and Filomena seemed to have been finalized with an unexpected suddenness that left him feeling slightly dazed. When Filomena made up her mind, she acted quickly. But she had been staying just out of reach for so long he was almost wary of accepting the reality of her surrender.

But a smart man didn't question good fortune when it came his way, Trent told himself. Filomena was here in his arms, and she was going to marry him. Surely that was all that mattered.

TWO DAYS LATER Shari's wedding went off like clockwork, which didn't surprise anyone who knew Meg Cromwell's talent for organization. Virtually everyone in town was invited and virtually everyone came. The reception was held at the country club, and the lavish buffet was replenished frequently to keep up with the throng of hungry guests.

An hour into the celebration, Filomena found a moment or two alone with her mother, who had been bustling about with tireless energy.

"Everything's perfect, Mom. You pulled it off beautifully. Don't Shari and Jim look terrific together?"

Meg nodded in maternal satisfaction as she gazed fondly at her statuesque blond daughter who was in the middle of a crowd. "Perfect. A lovely couple. And they're so happy. Jim's going to make Shari an excellent husband."

Filomena sipped her champagne. "I think you're right."

"Trent is going to make you an excellent husband, too, my dear. I'm so pleased things worked out between the two of you. I don't mind telling you I was a little nervous there for a while."

"Afraid I'd blow it, huh?" Filomena smiled over the rim of her glass.

"Well," Meg said bluntly, "you seemed to be doing your best to keep him at arm's length."

"He made me nervous," Filomena explained.

"Nervous! How on earth did he do that?" Meg looked and sounded shocked.

"I'm not sure. Maybe because deep down I knew I wouldn't be able to keep him at arm's length for very long, not if he decided to close the gap."

"Which he did, thank goodness," Meg concluded. "I just wish the two of you weren't going to rush the ceremony. Just think what a terrific job I could do on a second wedding now that I've had an opportunity to practice."

Filomena laughed. "Talk to Trent. He's the one who doesn't want to wait."

"Well, I suppose I can see his reasoning. He's waited long enough, hasn't he? And so have you, for that matter. High time both of you made a commitment. Life goes by so quickly, and sometimes we forget the important things, thinking there's going to be plenty of time."

"Trent said something about that, too."

"Well, it's the truth. The older you get, the more you realize it. Trent is a good man, Fil. You couldn't have found anyone better."

"I know." She paused and then said cautiously, "He's got a thing about honesty. Did you know that? He's rather unbending in some ways."

"So? Do you want a man who doesn't have a strong sense of integrity? Someone like Brady Paxton?" Meg demanded bracingly.

"Of course not." Filomena decided to change the topic. "Looks like everyone's here. Even Brady and his wife. I'm surprised they showed up."

Meg was mildly astonished. "Why wouldn't they show up? It would have looked very awkward if they hadn't. People would have talked, and I'm sure the Paxtons knew it."

"People were already talking about Brady and me, apparently."

"Don't be ridiculous. That sort of gossip came to a quick halt when you and Trent announced your engagement. Actually, I think it stopped before that. I didn't hear another word about you and Brady after you went to Portland with Trent. Thank goodness that man took the reins into his own hands. As I said, I was getting very worried."

"If I were you, I'd start worrying about Uncle George and Aunt Agnes." Filomena nodded meaningfully toward her relatives who were regaling a large group across the room with increasingly loud conversation. Gloria Paxton, dressed in an overly snug knit dress, was standing in the group. So was Trent. He seemed to be amused by whatever George was saying.

Instantly alarmed, Meg snapped her head around to pin down George and Agnes in the crowd. "What are those two up to now? I swear, Fil, if they make a scene this afternoon, I will personally murder both of them."

"They do seem to be getting a little loud. They're obviously having a good time."

"Oh, heavens, I'd better go put the lid on George before he gets up on a table or something. I must speak to your father about cutting off their champagne." Meg dashed into the crowd, the skirts of her mauve mother-of-the-bride dress swirling out behind her.

Filomena watched her mother for a moment and then turned with a small, private smile to help herself to another round of goodies from the buffet table. Uncle George's laughter sailed across the room. It faded a bit as Meg Cromwell joined the group. Filomena didn't envy her mother the task of keeping a lid on Uncle George. He was a big, boisterous man, and when he was in an expansive mood everyone around him knew it.

Filomena was taking a bite out of a cream cheese and shrimp canapé when she heard her uncle say something about a dowry. She paused, the cracker halfway into her mouth, and listened with a sense of startled surprise that rapidly turned into shock.

"Don't want anyone here to think we'd send our two nieces into marriage without a proper wedding gift," Uncle George declared loudly. He grinned first at Shari's new husband and then at Trent. "Agnes and I've been saving this announcement until now because we wanted it to be a surprise. Fact is, I bought some good land along the coast a few years back. Picked up two nice-sized tracts for a song. I told Agnes they'd be a heck of an investment, and I was right. As usual. I don't mind telling you all that both parcels are worth a tidy sum now. And Agnes and I are going to give each of our nieces a tract as wedding gifts. What do you think about that?" George and Agnes gazed around at the crowd with an expectant air.

They weren't disappointed. Everyone broke into hearty congratulations. The room was full of delighted comments and good wishes. Filomena could hear Shari exclaiming in amazement. Her husband looked startled but pleased. Filomena's parents were shaking their heads in wry, amused wonder.

But Filomena's gaze collided with Trent's in that moment, and she went cold inside.

He looked at her across the heads of the people separating them. There was no amusement in his eyes, no look of cheerful congratulations or delight in Shari's and Filomena's good fortune. There was, instead, a strange, forbidding anger. It was an expression unlike anything Filomena had ever seen in his gaze. It frightened her as nothing had frightened her in a very long time.

Filomena was filled with a sudden, sickening foreboding.

Trent glanced toward the patio and then back at her. The message was unmistakable. *Message, nothing*, she thought. It was an order. He wanted to talk to her out on the patio. She gave him a small, almost imperceptible nod and slowly started to make her way through the crowd.

But it wasn't Trent who was waiting for her near the open door. It was Gloria Paxton. Her face was flushed, and it was obvious she'd had a considerable amount of champagne. Her eyes were dangerously bright.

"Hello, Gloria, I hope you're enjoying yourself."

"Oh, I'm enjoying myself tremendously now that some very interesting questions have been answered."

"Good. Excuse me. I thought I'd get away from the noise for a while." Filomena tried to step around the other woman. Gloria allowed her to slip outside, but she followed hard on Filomena's heels.

"I see you didn't wear one of those tarty dresses you and your friend design." Gloria ran a disparaging eye over the discreetly cut, patterned yellow silk dress Filomena was wearing. "Decent of you not to cause a scene at your sister's wedding. I half expected you to show up in a harem outfit or a string bikini. But I guess your *fiancé* wouldn't approve of that, would he?"

Filomena counted slowly to ten and promised herself she wouldn't shove Gloria Paxton into the pool, at least not until Shari and Jim had left the reception. She owed her sister that much consideration. "If you don't mind, Gloria, I'd like a few minutes alone. It's been a hectic afternoon."

"Not just a hectic afternoon, a hectic vacation, right, Fil?" Gloria asked maliciously. "You certainly had your work cut out for you, didn't you? First you made a try for Brady. But that didn't get far, did it? He never did want you, Fil. It was me he wanted, right from the start. He was just killing time with you nine years ago."

"Gloria, I think we'd better put paid to this conversation before it gets any more embarrassing."

"Are you embarrassed, Fil? That's hard to believe. The last time you looked really embarrassed was when you walked in on Brady and me. I never told you I planned that little scene, did I? I knew you were on your way over to see Brady. I'd phoned your house to check. But I got to his place first and staged a big bedroom scene for your benefit. It worked like a charm. Brady had been stalling about breaking off your engagement, but after you found us he had to act."

Filomena sighed. "All that might have mattered once, but it doesn't anymore."

"I'll never forget the expression on your face. You looked like someone's pet dog whose master had just kicked it in the teeth. But you've turned into a real tough cookie since then, haven't you? You're a lot smarter now than you were in the old days. You came back here to see if you could get your claws into my husband, but you pulled off an even bigger coup when you tricked Trent Ravinder into proposing, didn't you?"

"Gloria, you don't know what you're talking about. I suggest you cut back on the champagne."

"Don't worry about me. Worry about yourself. Because this time I think you've bitten off more than you can chew. Ravinder is no fool, and now that he's found out you've played him for one he's not going to be pleased. He'll probably wring your neck."

Filomena, who had been on the point of turning away and walking back into the crowded room, stopped and stared at her, stunned. "What on earth are you talking about?" she asked. But she knew what Gloria was about to say.

"Don't look so stupid and innocent. That's the same dumb look you had on your face nine years ago. It won't wash, Fil. You're a big girl now and you know what you're doing. It's no secret any longer. We all heard what your generous Uncle George just said in there, didn't we? It's all clear now, Fil. I can see exactly what you've been planning."

"Is that right?" Filomena took a step toward Gloria. Her voice was too soft, but Gloria didn't seem to comprehend the significance of that. "Just what is it you think I've been planning?"

"It's obvious." Gloria waved her arm, and some of the champagne in her glass spilled over the rim. "You decided to find a way to collect that land your aunt and uncle planned to give you when you got married, didn't you? Your uncle's announcement explains everything. It was so touching to hear George and Agnes talk about their little 'surprise' wedding gifts for you and Shari, the two wonderful nieces who are almost like their own daughters." Gloria's mouth twisted savagely.

"You don't know what you're talking about."

But Gloria ignored Filomena's fierce protest. Her bitter gaze moved past Filomena to the man who had appeared in the doorway. She smiled grimly at Trent. "What about it, Trent? Weren't you amazed to learn that Filomena's going to receive that valuable land on the coast? And all she had to do to get it was get married. Lucky you came along, isn't it? I must admit, I'm glad you did. If you hadn't been available, she would have tried to take Brady. It's obvious she needed a man, any man, in order to get hold of that land."

Gloria's face crumpled in a combination of rage and tears. She flung aside her champagne glass and ran clumsily past Filomena and Trent. An instant later she disappeared into the crowded room.

Filomena turned slowly to confront a grim-faced Trent. She looked for amusement or indulgence or impatience in his expression and saw nothing. The jade-green eyes were totally unreadable. He was regarding her as if she were some new and unknown example of alien life form. A sick feeling washed over Filomena.

"Trent, please don't look at me that way," she begged.

"How should I look at you, Filomena?"

She shook her head frantically. "Why are you so upset about what my uncle just said?"

"How long have you known about the land, Fil?"

She looked at him helplessly. "I knew my aunt and uncle had a lot of real estate, but I didn't know they were going to use some of it as wedding gifts for Shari and me. What difference does it make, anyway? What's wrong? What are you thinking?"

"I'm thinking about how much you need a large chunk of cash to finance your ambitious expansion plans for Cromwell & Sterling, Inc. I'm remembering how disappointed you were when Glenna phoned the other day to tell you the bank had denied your application for a loan."

Filomena went pale. "Trent, you can't possibly think that I—"

"I'm remembering that it was right after you found out you weren't going to get the bank loan that you suddenly announced you were going to marry me. I'm thinking that there's a good explanation now for your sudden reversal of attitude on the subject of love and marriage. I wondered at the time why you changed your mind so quickly. I should have known my so-called victory came a little too easily."

"*Trent.*"

"So you tell me what's wrong, Filomena," he went on harshly. "Tell me all the reasons you suddenly changed your mind about marriage after nine years of declaring you had no interest in being a wife."

She fought for air, feeling faint for the first time in her life. This was worse than that horrible moment when she'd walked in on Brady and Gloria. A frenzied fear shafted through her. Her mind was already leaping ahead to the obvious conclusion to this terrible scene. *This couldn't be happening.* Not between her and Trent.

"You must know I can't prove anything," she said in a dry, agonized whisper. "My aunt and uncle are always pulling surprises out of the hat. I've known about their real estate investments for years."

"For nine years you've been more interested in your career than you have in marriage. Then one summer you suddenly need a lot of money for your all-important business plans. The bank loan falls through, but you're too damn proud and independent to ask a man for money. But there's no reason you shouldn't find a way to tap into your future, is there? Some day that land on the coast was going to be yours, anyway. Why not collect it now and sell it? Maybe you'd almost forgotten about that real estate over the years because you didn't want to pay the price of marriage to get it. But now you really could use the money. And marriage to me might not be so bad. After all, we're good in bed together, we have a lot in common and the family approves of me. And if it doesn't work out, what the hell? That's what divorce is for, right?"

"Stop it, Trent. Stop it right now. Don't say another word." Filomena clamped her hands over her ears in a futile effort to halt the inevitable.

He stepped forward and caught hold of her wrists, yanking her hands down to her sides. "Damn it, Filomena, what kind of a fool do you think I am?"

Filomena's temper exploded as it hadn't done since childhood. This time the result was far more cataclysmic because it contained the full power and fury of a woman, not just that of a young girl.

"Let go of me!" she snapped, jerking herself free of his hold. Trent was so startled by the abrupt, violent maneuver that he released her. She backed away from him. "You've got a hell of a nerve, you arrogant bastard. You demand trust from everyone else, including me. You insist on everyone respecting your honor and your word. You're so damn proud of your shining integrity. But you're not willing to put a little faith in someone else's honor, are you? Not even that of the woman you claim you love. I'm supposed to trust you implicitly, but apparently you don't have to trust me when the chips are down. Oh, no. I have to give you proof that I'm on the level."

"Filomena…" He started forward but halted when she held up her hands.

"Stop right there, Trent. Don't come any closer. I know what you're going to say."

"You think so?" he shot back, looking furious.

She nodded proudly. "Oh, yes. I know what comes next. You're going to break off the engagement, naturally. A man of your magnificent integrity, a man with your kind of honesty and pride, couldn't possibly marry a scheming little hussy like me. I realize that. Don't worry, I won't make a scene. I've lived through one broken engagement and I'll live through another. But this time around it's going to be different. Do you hear me?"

"Filomena, will you shut up?" he said through gritted teeth. "I've got a few more things to say."

"I don't want to hear them. I already know what you're going to say. But you can damn well wait until after my sister's wedding. Do you understand?" She drew herself up with fierce pride. "In fact, you can wait until after I'm out of this town. I won't go through it again. I will not be humiliated in front of everyone in Gallant Lake tonight the way I was nine years ago. I went through it once and I refuse to let another man do it to me again. I know you're going to break off the engagement. *But you will keep quiet about it until I'm out of this town.*"

"Damn it, Filomena!"

"You owe me that much, Trent," she reminded him tightly. "Remember? You owe me for the night I changed that dress. Since you're a man of such rock-hard integrity, I'm sure you wouldn't want to welsh on the deal. All I'm asking is for you to hold off breaking the engagement until I can get packed and leave for Seattle."

He reached for her then, but she was gone, slipping through his fingers before he could close them around her and hold her still.

Trent was left clutching a handful of air.

9

TRENT RAVINDER WAS TORN between hot fury and cold, clammy fear. He had never experienced such a volatile combination of emotions before in his life, and they left him feeling almost paralyzed. He stood at the edge of the crowd, his fingers locked in a death grip around a glass of champagne and watched Filomena dance with anyone who asked her.

She was never free for an instant. She flitted from one man to another, her eyes dangerously bright and her smile unnaturally brilliant. Her red hair swung free, a wave of fire down her back as she was whirled about the floor. The golden silk skirts of her dress whipped teasingly around her legs, and her silvery high-heeled sandals flashed in the light.

She was untouchable and unreachable even when one of her partners held her close in a slow dance. She was a glittering elfin queen, a creature of magic, a woman who shimmered and tantalized just beyond a man's reach.

For a little while he'd caught hold of her and kept her safe within the circle of his arms, Trent thought. But now she was trying to break free again. He sensed in the pit of his stomach that she was about to vanish in a puff of smoke.

It infuriated him that she assumed he was going to break off the engagement. The truth was he hadn't gotten that far in his thinking. He'd gone up in flames at the idea that she might have agreed to marry him just to get hold of that valuable land. But his anger hadn't taken him any farther than the immediate need to confront her and punish her in some way for trying to use him.

He was equally enraged to receive that lecture on trust and integrity. Who did she think she was to be lecturing him on the subject? She was the one whose ethics were in question here. She was the one who had apparently decided that after nine years of stating otherwise, marriage now would be financially convenient.

Trent's eyes narrowed as he watched another man swing Filomena out onto the dance floor. He wanted to shake her. He wanted to yell at her. He wanted her to learn that she couldn't use him, even if she did melt like warm honey in his arms. He wanted her desperately, but he wasn't about to let her get away with murder. Shari had warned him once that Filomena might try to run roughshod over him. Well, she was not going to succeed in treating him as a pleasant, useful toy. The elf had to learn the limits of the spells she cast over him.

But even while he told himself he was going to teach her a lesson, Ravinder wondered at the anguish and the sense of betrayal he had seen in her eyes when she had told him he must not break the engagement until she was out of town.

On top of everything else Trent was infuriated by the idea that Filomena thought he would humiliate her at her own sister's wedding. She should know him better than that. She should have trusted him. This business about the land was between the two of them; it didn't involve anyone else.

But the moment he had turned on her, angry and accusing, she'd immediately leaped to the conclusion that he was rejecting her. And she was sure he was going to do it right then and there in front of most of Gallant Lake, Oregon.

Just as Brady Paxton had rejected her so long ago.

The thought chilled Trent. He would never have hurt her like that. He loved her. And when she sorted out her priorities she would find out that she loved him, too. But damned if he was going to let her marry him just because it was financially convenient. He'd waited too long, searched too hard and fallen too much in love with Filomena Cromwell to allow her to do that to him.

Trent got a grip on his raging temper and made himself plan. He would marry Filomena, but it would be on his terms. She could kiss her aunt and uncle's wedding gift goodbye or put it in trust for the children. He didn't care what she did with it as long as she didn't use it to expand Cromwell & Sterling. Filomena was going to have to prove to him that she was marrying for love.

Out on the dance floor Filomena alighted like a butterfly on the arm of yet another man. Trent instinctively took a step forward, part of him wanting to snatch her away from her new partner. He hated to see another man's hands on her, even in the formal embrace of a dance. They had things to settle, he and Filomena. She wasn't going to get away with avoiding him like this.

He halted, frustrated and angry when the dance swept her out of reach. If he went after her now, he would cause a scene that would probably turn into a local legend. Filomena would never forgive him.

Seething with fury, Trent stayed where he was. The wedding reception couldn't last forever. He was spoiling for a fight, but he could wait until after the reception when he would be able to corner Filomena.

But half an hour later when the bride and bridegroom departed, Filomena did, too. By the time Trent realized she had left the country club, it was too late. By the time he got back to the lodge, she had left town.

He stormed into the bedroom she had been using and found it bare except for one silver high-heeled sandal that had apparently gotten pushed under the bed and overlooked in the hasty packing process.

Trent stood in the middle of the empty room holding the silver sandal and decided he didn't feel like Prince Charming after the ball.

THREE DAYS LATER Filomena returned from grocery shopping with an armful of packages bearing Pike Place Market labels. The phone was ringing in her apartment as she juggled a long loaf of French bread, a sack containing fat, fresh peaches and plump blueberries and a package of freshly made ravioli.

Filomena listened with dread to the imperious ringing of the phone as she halted in front of her apartment door and fished out her keys. She wasn't eager to answer the summons. With a little luck the caller might give up before she got inside the door. Every time the phone had rung since her return from Gallant Lake, she had been certain it would be her mother and father calling to express their shock over the broken engagement.

Filomena didn't want to deal with the inevitable postmortems, though sooner or later she knew she would have to do so. She kept telling herself she just needed a little more time to regain her emotional equilibrium, but the truth was she didn't seem to be making much progress in that direction. Her moods swung wildly from a numb depression to a blazing fury that showed few signs of abating.

During the first twenty-four hours after she'd returned from Gallant Lake, Filomena hadn't answered the phone at all. She had huddled in the safety of her apartment the way a small animal huddles in its burrow while waiting for the shadow of the predator to pass.

The following day she had recovered enough to be angry with herself for her lack of spirit. She was no vulnerable, naive nineteen-year-old hovering on the brink of adulthood. She was a mature, successful, self-confident woman, and she would not let any man do this to her, least of all a hypocritical, arrogant bastard who had only wanted to marry her in the first place because he had decided it was time to find a wife.

She had blotted up the last of her tears and gone for a walk. It wasn't much, but it was a start. At least it had gotten her out of the apartment. When she returned, she found the courage to start answering the phone again. No one who knew anything about the Gallant Lake fiasco had called, however. She wondered at the silence from her parents but decided to be grateful for small favors. She didn't question the silence from Trent Ravinder. She assumed he had no wish to speak to her again.

The bastard.

The phone shrilled its summons as Filomena fumbled with the key and opened the door. It was still ringing by the time she had set down her packages and grabbed for the red instrument.

"Hello?" Filomena's voice was cautious but firm.

"Fil? Is that you? What's wrong? You sound strange."

Filomena relaxed. "Hi, Glenna. How did you know I was home?"

"I called your parents' place in Gallant Lake. Your mother said she thought you were here in Seattle. What's going on? I thought you were going to take another couple of weeks to unwind in bucolic splendor."

"Bucolic splendor gets boring after a while. How are things going?"

"Okay. I was just calling to tell you I've filled out a couple more loan applications, but I'll need your signature before I turn them into the bank. I was going to express-mail them to Gallant Lake, but since you're in town I guess it won't be a problem."

Filomena glanced at her watch. "It's too late to do anything about them today. I'll come by the office tomorrow and sign them. Thanks for doing all the paperwork, Glenna."

"No problem. That first loan form we did together was the hardest. I'm feeling more hopeful now than I was a few days ago when the first bank turned us down. I guess this is what being entrepreneurs is all about. Lots of highs and lows."

"I hate being dependent on banks," Filomena muttered.

"So do I. But since neither one of us has won the lottery recently, there's not much else we can do. How else can we get hold of the kind of money it takes to expand?"

"Good question," Filomena said wryly. She supposed Trent would have had a few nasty comments to make on that subject. "I'll see you bright and early in the morning."

"Right." Glenna hung up the phone.

Filomena did the same but more slowly. She stood gazing unseeingly at the view of Mount Rainier that was framed in the angled window of her corner apartment and wondered how long it was going to be before she recovered her enthusiasm for Cromwell & Sterling's ambitious plans. Somehow it was hard to feel enthusiastic about anything today.

It wasn't until she turned to head back to the kitchen to unpack her groceries that she realized she wasn't alone in the apartment. Too late she remembered she had left the door open in her haste to get to the phone. A wave of cold terror raced through her as she whirled around to confront the intruder.

Trent Ravinder was lounging in the open doorway. He was wearing the kind of clothes he'd worn in Gallant Lake: a pair of jeans, a plaid shirt and low boots. His arms were folded across his chest, and he was watching her with an unwavering regard. The shock of seeing him held Filomena speechless for several seconds.

"You shouldn't leave the door open behind you when you come home, Filomena," he remarked coolly. "No telling who might decide to follow you inside."

"I can see the problem," she managed through dry lips. "What do you want, Trent?"

He came through the door, shutting it behind him. "That's obvious, isn't it? I came to finish the conversation we started at your sister's wedding reception. You skipped out on me before we could conclude it."

Tension ripped through her, driving out the misery and replacing it with a surge of white-hot anger. "There was nothing left to say. You said it all." She glanced down at her bare hands and then raised her eyes back to his. "We never got around to buying rings, so I don't have one to return."

"You're so sure I want to end the engagement, aren't you?" He shoved his hands into his back pockets and began stalking through her living room.

Filomena resented the way he eyed everything with deep curiosity, as if he had a right to investigate her secrets. He looked huge in the room, dwarfing her chic, trendy furnishings. "Of course I assumed you wanted to end the engagement," she snapped. "Why would you want to marry a conniving, money-hungry woman like me? And why haven't you told my parents that we're through?"

He stopped to examine a whimsically designed one-legged counter stool that looked as if it would collapse if he were to sit on it. "I haven't told your parents that we're through because we aren't through."

She drew a deep steadying breath. "I don't understand, Trent."

"I know you don't. You're so busy worrying about how to handle the big rejection scene that you haven't given much thought to the fact that I haven't actually rejected you."

"At least you didn't do it in front of all those people at my sister's wedding reception," she shot back bitterly. "I guess I should thank you for that much."

"I didn't do it then and I'm not doing it now because as far as I'm concerned we're still engaged."

"That doesn't make any sense, Trent. Why would you want to marry me? You're convinced I was using you to get my hands on some convenient money."

He looked at her from across the room, his green eyes brilliant and unrelenting. "Were you?"

"No, damn it! I was not using you. I had no idea my aunt and uncle were going to give Shari and me such valuable wedding gifts. I agreed to marry you because I wanted to marry you. There was no other reason."

"Prove it."

She stared at him uncomprehendingly. "What?"

"I've given this a lot of thought, Filomena," Trent said coolly. "And I'm prepared to let you prove that your intentions were sincere."

"How terribly decent of you," she replied scathingly. "Just how am I supposed to do that?"

"Simple. You can either refuse the gift or put the land in trust for our own children. I don't care what you do with it as long as you don't use it to finance Cromwell & Sterling's expansion plans."

She could hardly believe her ears. Fury welled up in her again, as fresh as it had been three days ago. "How dare you." Her voice was a tight whisper. "How *dare* you. I don't have to prove a thing to you, you big, arrogant bull moose. If anyone should be trying to prove something, it's you. You're the one who's demonstrating about as much trust as a rabbit for a snake. What makes you think I would want to marry a man who had so little faith in me, let alone prove anything to him?"

"Three days ago you said you loved me."

"That was three days ago. I'm a lot older and wiser now."

He took a step toward her, his features harsh and rigid in the late afternoon light. "Is that right? You find it that easy to fall out of love? Then what's the big deal about being afraid I'd announce the end of the engagement before you got a chance to clear out of town? If you didn't love me in the first place, why worry about calling off the marriage?"

Filomena found herself retreating a step as Trent came toward her. Her emotions were in a chaotic jumble. She wanted to yell, and at the same time she wanted to cry. It was too much. He had no right to do this to her. She was the innocent victim here, not him. "I had no desire to be humiliated by another man in front of the entire population of Gallant Lake. Can't you understand that?"

"I didn't humiliate you. You're the one who was going to humiliate me by combining marriage plans with business plans. If we're going to talk about humiliation, why don't we discuss it from my angle?"

"Your angle! Shall I tell you how it looks from *my* angle? It looks to me as if you had simply made an intellectual, pragmatic, businesslike decision to get married this year because you had decided it was time you had a wife. I came along at the appropriate moment, and the next thing I know I'm engaged to you. How should I interpret that? Certainly not as the great romantic love story of the year. It looks a lot more like a convenient, businesslike arrangement to me."

"You're the one who announced the engagement, or have you forgotten how you cheerfully informed Paxton that you were going to marry me? It seems to me I was one hell of a gentleman to back you up after you'd gotten yourself out on a very shaky limb."

"Why you big, overgrown, insensitive Neanderthal! You told me you loved me."

"So what? You told me you loved me."

"I *did* love you. I would never have agreed to marry you otherwise," she stormed. She was still retreating in the face of his steady advance, but she had reached the end of the line. She came up against the counter that separated the kitchen from the living area and found herself unable to retreat any farther. Tears stung her eyes; rage and pain combined and burned in a white-hot flame. Her hand swept out, and her fingers closed around a napkin holder. "Stay away from me."

"Why should I stay away from you? We're lovers." He moved closer.

"We're not anymore."

"Are you going to tell me you've fallen out of love with me already? In only three days' time?"

"Don't put words in my mouth!" She flung the napkin holder at him. He ducked the small missile. Behind him peach-colored paper napkins cascaded over the white carpet as the holder landed harmlessly.

"Tell me you've stopped loving me," Trent taunted, closing in on her. "Tell me you don't want me anymore. Tell me you want to end the engagement."

"I never said any of those things. *You* said them." She scrabbled along the countertop and found a small woven basket full of bottles of vitamin tablets. She hurled the basket at his head. Trent impatiently knocked it aside. The bottles clattered on the carpet.

"I never said those things, either," Trent reminded her forcefully as he closed the gap between them. "You assumed I was going to say them so you tried to vanish. But it won't work, elf. You're not pulling any of your magic disappearing acts with me."

"Get out of here." Filomena edged along the counter, seeking another weapon. "I mean it, Trent. You have no right to barge in like this after what you said to me in Gallant Lake."

"I've got every right. I'm engaged to you." He caught her wrist just as she was about to throw a pencil holder at him. His fingers tightened on her as he crowded her up against the counter. "And what's more, I think you're still in love with me. You just need to get your priorities straight. I thought I had your full attention after that night in Portland, but there were still a few distractions left, weren't there, Filomena? You still had other things on your mind besides me. But I think deep down you do love me, and you're going to prove it to me and to yourself."

"Your ego has to be seen to be believed! Why should I bother to prove anything to you, you big buffalo?" She struggled against his hold, but it was useless. He wasn't being rough with her, but that didn't change the fact that she couldn't move. He held her with a casual, gentle strength that was overwhelming.

"Forget the rest of it, Filomena," he ordered softly. "Forget the fear of being rejected, forget the expansion plans for Cromwell & Sterling, forget the arguments about trust and just tell me the truth. Do you love me?"

"What do you care?" she wailed.

"I care," he said simply, and bent his head to capture her mouth.

Filomena struggled against the marauding kiss for a full minute, but it was useless. Her only real defense would be to go limp in his arms, but there was no chance of that. Her own emotions were burning too fiercely to allow her to react with any degree of restraint. She was too wound up, too alive with the vibrant, dangerous sensations he aroused in her. She had to react somehow, in a direct, physical way.

She couldn't fight him. The hold he had on her wouldn't permit it. Instead, all the pent-up anger and desperation transmuted into a raging desire that sent shudders through her.

"That's it, sweetheart," he breathed in deep satisfaction. "Show me how you really feel."

"You arrogant, oversized, bullheaded—"

"Hush," he advised, dragging his mouth across hers to ensure she obeyed. "Don't talk. This isn't the time. We'll talk later."

"Mmmmph." She felt his teeth nipping gently on her lower lip as he swung her up into his arms and started down the hall to the bedroom. She clung to him, aware of the fire in her veins and the hard muscled wall of his chest. She tried to think clearly, but she couldn't. Nothing mattered now that he was here and telling her he wanted her.

Trent carried her into the light turquoise and salmon-pink bedroom and dropped her into the center of the quilted bed. Before she could move he came down on top of her, crushing her into the blue-green bedding. He sprawled over her, anchoring her securely beneath him.

"Show me," he muttered against her throat. "Show me that nothing has changed between us when it comes to this."

She cried out softly, whispering his name over and over as he stripped off her shirt and trousers with sure, possessive hands. A moment later she was naked, twisting impatiently in his arms as he lifted himself away from her long enough to shrug out of his own clothes.

"You're so sweet and soft," he said wonderingly as he stroked her curving thigh. "Once I get past the thorns there's nothing but silk and velvet petals. Every time I see you walk across a room I want to touch you. I want to run my hands through your hair and feel you shiver and turn to me. I want to see you smile at me and reach for me as if there were no one and nothing else in the whole world that mattered. Do you understand?"

"I understand." She did because that was the way she felt about him, Filomena realized. She touched him gently, running her fingertips down his chest to the hard planes of his bare hip. He was fully aroused, heavy and warm with the need that was pulsing through him. When she hesitantly moved her hand to the hard shaft of his manhood, he groaned and murmured hot, exciting words of desire in her ear.

Filomena grew bolder, cupping him gently and stroking him until he caught her hand and uttered a shaky laugh.

"That's enough for now, sweetheart. Any more and I'll explode. I want you so much. I've been going crazy during the past three days."

"Why did you wait to come after me if you . . . if you still wanted me?" she asked softly.

"I figured we both needed time to cool down." He grazed the tip of her breast with his thumb until the nipple hardened. Then he lowered his head and tasted the small, taut berry.

Filomena moaned and lifted one leg to curve around his thigh. She wrapped her arms around his neck and moved her hips invitingly against him. "Oh, Trent . . ."

"I know, sweetheart, I know. This part was never in doubt, was it?" He didn't wait for an answer. Instead he began trailing hot, damp kisses over her breasts and down her stomach. When she gasped and dug her nails into him, he groaned thickly. Then he let her feel his teeth on the soft, sensitive skin of her inner thigh. Filomena tightened her hold on him, pleading for him to complete the embrace.

"Now," she begged, "love me now, Trent."

"I will, darling. Open yourself for me. Show me how much you want me. I've missed you so."

She obeyed, parting her legs and reaching out to pull him close. He shifted his weight, centering himself over her. Then she could feel him pushing boldly against her, invading her softness with a gentle aggression that was unbelievably exciting.

"Trent."

"Say it," he muttered hoarsely as he drove himself slowly, surely into her. "Tell me you love me."

"I love you."

"Again."

"*I love you.* Oh, Trent, how could you have doubted it?"

He didn't answer that. He sank himself completely into her, pausing briefly while they both adjusted to the intimate connection. Filomena could feel the rigid sexual tension in him. When her nails curved into his hips, he groaned and began the deep, pulsing rhythm.

"Wrap yourself around me," he said into her mouth. "Put your legs around me and hold me. Show me how much you want me, elf. No tricks, no games and no disappearing acts. Show me you want me." His tongue surged into her mouth as she obeyed.

Filomena gave herself up to the enthralling embrace, lost in the spiral of desire that was consuming them both. She loved him, even if she was still furious with him. *She loved him.*

Something began to tighten within Filomena, threatening to shatter her, and then the culmination of the lovemaking swept over her with the inevitable impact of a freight train. She cried out again, whispering Trent's name over and over as the tension within her was released in a thousand glittering shards. She heard her name in a muffled shout as Trent followed her into the cascading release, and then there was nothing but silence in the room.

A long time later Filomena shifted slightly, pleasantly aware of Trent's weight along the length of her. He still lay in a careless sprawl that covered her completely. When he felt her small movement, he lifted his head from her breast and looked down at her with lazy satisfaction.

"Am I getting heavy?"

She smiled. "You aren't *getting* heavy. You were born heavy."

"I foresee a lifetime of size jokes. You've called me everything from a bull moose to a tank." He dusted a small kiss across the top of her nose. "Luckily for you I don't take offense easily."

Her smile faded. "I wouldn't say that. You were very quick to take offense at my sister's wedding when you heard about the gift my aunt and uncle are planning to give me."

Trent shrugged. "That was different. More importantly, it's no longer an issue, is it?"

She saw the cool challenge in his expression and summoned up all her courage. "No," Filomena agreed, "it's not an issue. Not any longer."

"You'll put the land in trust or tell your aunt and uncle you don't want it?"

"I'll make it much simpler than that. I won't marry you in the first place."

"Filomena!" Shock and outrage flared in his eyes. His fingers, which had been absently massaging her arms, suddenly sank into her flesh.

Filomena flinched at the pressure, but her eyes never wavered. "Don't worry, Trent, I'm not going to deny either of us in a . . . a physical sense."

"What the hell's that supposed to mean?" he asked in a voice that was just one degree short of explosion.

She swallowed and forced herself to explain. "I'm suggesting we have an affair while we find out just how serious you are about love and marriage and the trust that goes with it. You wanted me to prove my love? All right, I'm prepared to do that. My way."

"What the devil do you think you're doing?" he demanded tightly.

"You're not the only one who needs some proof," she said quietly. "After that little scene at Shari's wedding, I need some proof, too. I'd like to be certain I'm marrying a man who knows how to give trust as well as demand it. I want a man who believes in me. I'd also like to be sure you're not marrying me just because I came along at the point in your life when you decided it would be nice to have a wife. I'd like to be sure I'm not just a solution to some mid-life crisis you're going through."

10

TWO WEEKS LATER Trent lounged in a deep chair and nursed a beer while he morosely regarded his ex-fiancée from the opposite side of a small cocktail table. Around them the friendly, trendy tavern filled up with the usual Friday afterwork crowd. Trent, who had just put in nearly four hours on the freeway from Portland, listened to his companion's enthusiastic conversation and decided that nothing had proven more frustrating in his life than an affair with Filomena Cromwell.

He must have been out of his mind to let himself get maneuvered into this ridiculous situation. Looking back, he still wasn't quite certain how it had happened, but he was beginning to suspect that pride was the main problem.

Filomena's feminine pride was proving every bit as stubborn and intransigent as his own male version. He should have guessed it would, he thought moodily. The woman had had experience in using pride as a barrier against humiliation and defeat. She also had plenty of experience using it to keep men at bay.

She was bright and cheerful this evening, high on the results of her meeting with the business consultant Trent had sent her and Glenna to during the week. Cromwell & Sterling was apparently going to pursue a safer and less ambitious development plan thanks to the advice of the consultant.

"He made a lot of sense, Trent. It was obvious he'd really spent some time with our financial statement, and he spent a lot of time with Glenna and me just talking about where we really wanted to go. Then he had us sit down and make out a five-year plan. It forced us to be realistic and to think through some things we hadn't worried too much about until now. He agreed with your diagnosis that Cromwell & Sterling is at a very vulnerable stage of its development. We simply can't afford to take too many risks just now. A major disaster could wipe us out. We need some steady, sustained growth, not a flashy leap that might take us over the edge of a cliff." Filomena smiled at him. "Glenna and I really appreciate your setting up that meeting with Mr. Handel. With his advice under our belts, we'll be in much better shape to approach the banks again in a few months."

"I'm glad it worked out." Trent had to get the brief response in quickly before Filomena launched into another topic. Her generous thanks was unexpected. It helped lift his mood.

"I was very impressed by the way he researched the apparel trade before our meeting. He was far more knowledgeable than I expected him to be, and he seemed to know how active Seattle is in the clothing industry these days. Turns out he had consulted with another local sportswear firm a few months ago."

"Terrific."

She missed the sarcasm entirely, racing into a blow-by-blow description of the five-year plan she and Glenna had concocted and a detailed outline of the changes and modifications they had made in it under Handel's advice.

Trent made one or two other short responses during the next twenty minutes but decided Filomena probably wouldn't have noticed if he hadn't said a word. It had been like this for the past two weeks, ever since that afternoon in her bedroom when she'd announced she wouldn't marry a man who didn't trust her.

Now, whenever he was with her, she was bright, breezy and occasionally infuriating. Much of the time she was staying just out of reach again, baiting him, tantalizing him, slipping away from him whenever he tried to pin her down. In some ways their relationship now resembled the one they'd had during the early days in Gallant Lake, except for the fact that they were sleeping together.

Trent couldn't take a great deal of comfort from that because having an affair meant he was only seeing Filomena on the weekends and occasionally during the week. That hadn't been his intention at all. He wanted her as his wife, and she knew it. It seemed to him she was deliberately going out of her way to make him aware of what he was missing. She needn't have bothered. Every night during the week when he got into an empty bed he knew what he was missing.

He still didn't understand exactly what had gone wrong, but he was beginning to realize he should have made more allowance for Filomena's pride and her accompanying desire for revenge. She was making him pay for the demands he had made regarding that damn tract of land her aunt and uncle planned to give her.

Trent had hoped that once Handel had talked Cromwell & Sterling into slowing down their expansion plans, Filomena would realize she didn't need the land. But even if she had realized it, the knowledge hadn't done him any good. Unfortunately Filomena was now defending a principle.

So was he.

"Doesn't sound like you'll need the big bank loan," Trent managed to insert when Filomena finally wound down for a few seconds.

"No, at least not right away. Handel convinced us that our plans to open our own outlets were a few years too early."

Trent took a deep breath. "Then that makes the business of the wedding gift from your aunt and uncle a nonissue."

She gave him a sharp look. "I didn't say Cromwell & Sterling couldn't use an influx of cash. We still have growth plans, Trent, even if they're not quite as ambitious as they were before. We're going to go ahead and start a line for women who are on the other side of the average range."

An angry impatience flared in him. "You're saying you'd still like to get your hands on that land then?"

"What's wrong with being practical?"

"You're driving a wedge between us by being so damned practical."

"You're the one who turned it into a major blockbuster of an issue."

Trent took a firm grip on his temper. He knew she was baiting him, and it irritated him to know she could get a rise out of him so easily. "What are your plans for us?"

She looked at him over the rim of her wineglass. "I have no immediate plans. Why do you ask?"

"Because I want to get married." He set the beer mug down onto the table much too loudly. Several heads turned to glance in his direction. Trent ignored them. He leaned forward and pinned Filomena with his eyes. "What's more, you know it. You're deliberately tormenting me, trying to punish me for having the nerve to ask you not to accept your aunt's and uncle's gift."

"I have no intention of marrying a man who doesn't trust me. This time around it's money. What if it was something else next time? What if it was another man, Trent? Hmm? What would you do if you suspected I might be seeing another man? How would you make me prove my innocence? Force me to walk across a bed of hot coals? Forget it."

The thought of Filomena with another man sent a cold, tight sensation through his belly. Trent leaned even closer, pitching his words low across the small space that separated him from Filomena. "If I thought you were making a fool out of me by seeing another man, hot coals would be the least of your problems. I told you once I'm good at revenge. I'm also good at holding on to what belongs to me."

She sat back quickly in her chair, watching him carefully. Then she appeared to decide he wasn't quite as dangerous as he sounded. "Don't threaten me, Trent," she said bravely.

"I'm not threatening you. I'm making a statement of fact."

She waved that aside, obviously eager to take the argument in a new direction. "I'll have an affair with you as long as you want to have one, but until I'm convinced you really trust me I'm not about to get married. Now what shall we do about dinner? There's a new restaurant on First Avenue near the Pike Place Market. Want to try it?"

"Don't you dare try to switch the conversation like that. We were talking about our future."

"At the moment I'm not willing to look any farther into our future than dinner."

"It's your damn pride that's doing this to us," he informed her.

"I see the problem as being your pride, not mine," she shot back. "If you hadn't gone up in flames the second you heard about that land, we wouldn't be in this mess."

"Can you blame me for thinking you might have decided to marry me because you wanted that land? Everyone assured me you didn't have any interest in marriage and then, in a matter of days, you're suddenly telling an old boyfriend you plan to marry me. You've got to admit that's a fairly quick change of heart from a confirmed lady bachelor."

"I fell in love with you!"

"I believe you."

"You didn't the night of my sister's wedding reception."

"That's not true," Trent said through set teeth. "I believed you loved me then. I just wasn't sure if that was the reason you were marrying me. I wasn't positive you *knew* you loved me."

"Now you're saying you don't think I know my own mind?"

"I wanted to be married for the right reasons, not because the property and I came together as a nice, neat, convenient package."

"So it's *your* pride that's causing the problem," she flung back, "not mine."

There were several seconds of tense silence as they faced each other across the small table. "One of us," Trent finally said with a cold, calm logic that amazed him, "is going to have to back down or we'll drive each other insane. We can't go on like this."

"Fine. I'll agree to marry you as long as you make no stipulations about the land my aunt and uncle plan to give me."

"You don't need that land. You said so yourself."

"I need some proof that you trust me, really trust me. I want to be sure you believe I'm marrying you because I love you and not because you and the land make a financially convenient package. You're very quick to demand trust from others. Your word is your bond and all that. Well, I have a right to make certain you can extend trust. I need to know you're not going to doubt my love when the going gets rough."

"It's not your love I'm doubting. It's your common sense. How can you do this to us, Filomena? You're making both of us miserable. I'm not asking that much of you when I ask you to get rid of the land. Hell, if it's cash you need, I'll give it to you."

Fury leaped in her eyes, and then unexpectedly she suddenly seemed to weary of the battle. The spark went out of her expression, and her slender body wilted slightly. The change in her was unsettling. Trent realized he wasn't accustomed to the sight of Filomena giving up in the midst of a battle. It bothered him.

"You don't even realize what you're really asking. You want me to prove my love. Do you realize how truly arrogant that is, Trent?"

He sucked in his breath and closed his eyes for a grim moment. "Put like that, it does sound arrogant, doesn't it?" When he opened his eyes she was watching him with a disarmingly hopeful expression. The bright challenge had snapped back into her eyes the instant she sensed an opening. The lady made a wily opponent. He smiled sardonically, fully aware of what was going through her head.

"Well?" she prompted gently.

He sipped his beer. "Well, what?"

"Are you going to lower your pride and drop your demands concerning that land?"

"No," he said calmly, his temper back under control. He pulled out his wallet to pay the tab, aware that Filomena was staring at him in shock. She didn't know him very well if she thought she'd won that easily.

"Why not?" she demanded, all the fire returning to her expression. "Why can't you forget that bullheaded pride of yours long enough to let us patch up this quarrel?"

"Because," he said, laying out dollar bills, "the result of this quarrel, as you call it, is too important to me. Let's go try out that new restaurant you suggested." He stood up and reached for her hand to pull her to her feet.

"Trent, wait a minute!"

"Relax, Filomena. When I first met you, I told myself I'd give you time to realize what you really wanted. The whole summer, in fact, if that's what it takes. We've still got a few weeks left. Right now I'm hungry. Let's eat."

"But, Trent, I want to talk about this."

"You didn't a minute ago." He caught her arm and steered her toward the door.

"That was different."

"Has it ever struck you, Filomena, that you have a definite streak of contrariness?" Trent asked pleasantly.

"It probably goes with the red hair," she said in forbidding tones.

"That," he stated roughly, "is not an excuse."

When the weekend drew to a close, Trent told himself he had reason to be proud. The running battle with Filomena was far from over, but at least he had managed to ensure that it was fought more or less on his terms.

She tried again and again to draw him out into a full-blown argument where she could hurl the issue of his lack of trust in his face. Trent avoided the battles largely by changing the subject. He held his own impatience and temper severely in check, hoping that Filomena would eventually run out of fuel for the fight.

She danced around him all weekend, taunting him, baiting him, challenging him, searching for a way to make him retract his demand. Trent pretended to be unaware of the various tactics, contenting himself with taking passionate revenge in bed. It was the one place she didn't try to fight him. When it came to the passionate side of their relationship, she surrendered with so much excitement and fire and sensual generosity that Trent forgot all about winning and losing. He took everything she offered, glorying in it, and gave back all he had.

Sunday afternoon, when he prepared to leave for Portland, however, it was evident that Filomena wasn't about to surrender anything outside the bedroom. Her elfin face was as determined as ever, her eyes as bright and challenging. She kissed him farewell, drawing out the embrace until she sensed his body tightening with arousal. Then she drew back slightly and looked up at him.

"Trent, please think about what you're doing. You were right when you said we can't go on like this. We have to get this matter settled, or it will tear us apart."

Aware of the ache in his lower body, Trent sighed and cradled Filomena's face in his hands. When she smiled tremulously up at him, her eyes lighting with expectant hope, he shook his head slowly. "If you want to end it, you'll have to give me your word you'll get rid of the land." When she started to protest, he silenced her with a quick, possessive kiss. "Do it, Filomena," he ordered softly.

"Why should I?" she wailed.

"Because I'm going to win this battle. I always win when the issue is important to me."

"I won't marry a man who demands that I prove my love," she said flatly. "I won't marry a man who doesn't trust me."

"And I won't marry a woman who isn't willing to prove that she wants me more than a hunk of real estate." He leaned down and kissed her again and then he walked out the door.

It wasn't easy.

Three evenings later Trent sat alone in his darkened living room and stared out at the lights of Portland. He sipped morosely at a beer and wondered if he was pushing Filomena too hard.

She was inclined to be reckless when she was backed into a corner. She was also inclined to defend a position to the last gasp. She hadn't gotten where she was in the business world by being overly cautious or timid.

When it came to men she had little reason to be trusting, even less reason to want to prove herself. The problem wasn't just her bad experience with Brady Paxton. According to Shari, it also included the fact that she had apparently run into a few fortune hunters since Cromwell & Sterling had become successful. Given her background, she probably thought she had every right to demand that a man prove himself first.

On top of everything else, she had a certain, definite taste for revenge. He'd seen ample evidence of that during those hectic weeks of trying to keep an eye on her in Gallant Lake. If he pushed her far enough, there was no telling what she might do.

Trent thought about that raw fact while he downed the remainder of the beer.

THURSDAY MORNING Filomena sat with Glenna in an espresso café near the waterfront and tried valiantly to keep her mind on business. She and Glenna were supposed to be discussing designs for a new collection of sportswear based on a fabulous print fabric Filomena had located on her last trip to Italy. Filomena had bought up a huge quantity of it and had shipped it back to the States, even though at the time she hadn't been certain what she and Glenna would do with it. Glenna had loved the material as soon as she had seen it, however, and had immediately set about creating designs that would take full advantage of the dramatic pattern.

"I think we should do skirts and blouses in the print and use emerald green and coral silk for the contrast pieces," Glenna was saying enthusiastically as she handed Filomena some sketches. "What do you think of these?"

Filomena studied the dashing renditions of a trumpet skirt and a dropped shoulder blouse. "They look wonderful, Glenna. What do you think of a vest that could coordinate with the pants and the skirts? Something dressy maybe, with a little metallic dazzle in it?"

"Umm, good idea. We're taking a chance on this particular shade of coral and green, you know. They're exotics. They could fall flat next season if everyone's going back to beiges and mauve."

"We've made our reputation on exotics for petite women. They're just beginning to feel adventurous in our clothes. I wouldn't want to pull back now."

Glenna, who was barely five foot two, grinned. "I agree. Okay, we'll go for it." She picked up her cup of caffè latte and took a sip. The amusement faded from her eyes. "Speaking of exotics . . ."

Filomena raised her eyebrows. "What about them?"

"I was wondering how things are going with that rather large specimen you brought back from Gallant Lake."

"Don't ask."

"Why not?" Glenna's gaze was sympathetic. "I had the impression that this time around it might be for real."

"You're an incurable romantic, Glenna."

"And you're not? Come on, that's the whole problem, isn't it? Are you still holding out for that chunk of land your aunt and uncle want to give you as a wedding present?"

"Yes."

"You don't care about that land, Fil, and you know it."

"That's not the point," Filomena said patiently. "I have to know Trent trusts me. When he went through the roof after he heard about my aunt's and uncle's plans, I knew we had some major, unresolved difficulties in our relationship."

"You mean he put down his foot and you drew a line and dared him to step over it." Glenna shook her head. "I don't know, Fil. He's got awfully big feet."

Filomena raised her eyes to the ceiling in an expression of frustrated disgust. "You're not the only one to remark on that fact," she muttered, remembering her sister's comments on the subject. "Why does everyone assume that I'm the one who's going to have to back down? Why does everyone automatically leap to the conclusion that Trent will always get his way?"

"Maybe it has something to do with the fact that he could pick you up with one hand and carry you off over his shoulder if you give him too much trouble."

"As I've pointed out to Trent in the past, might does not make right."

"I have the feeling he's not going to surrender, Fil."

"It's not a question of surrender! It's a question of learning to trust. He's so damn autocratic and arrogant about his own integrity, Glenna, you wouldn't believe it. He'd probably fight duels with anyone who doubted his honor if it were still possible to do so. Trent is absolutely rigid when it comes to his own code. Everything is black and white. He doesn't allow any shades of gray."

"He sees that land your aunt and uncle want to give you as a gray area, huh?"

Filomena nodded. "And instead of giving me the benefit of the doubt, he wants me to get rid of it entirely. Imagine him having the nerve to ask me to make that kind of sacrifice!"

Glenna gave her a thoughtful glance. "All right, I can understand you're not exactly thrilled with the idea of having to prove yourself to him, but there's something more involved, isn't there? You love the man. I can tell. You've never been like this with anyone else in all the time I've known you. Why won't you give in on this issue?"

Filomena drew a weary breath. "You want the truth? I'm afraid to give in, Glenna. I'm afraid to marry a man who demands proof of my integrity. We're talking about a piece of real estate this time. What will it be next time? How many times will I have to prove myself to him? And what happens the first time I can't produce proof?"

Glenna's eyes widened with understanding. "I think I'm beginning to see the full scope of the problem. What if . . . what if he thought you were cheating on him with another man or something?"

Filomena nodded bleakly. "Exactly. Sooner or later we'd come up against a situation in which Trent would simply have to take my word. He'd have to trust me completely. I'm not sure he can do that. He's been so busy establishing his own credentials in that department that he's never had to learn to trust anyone else."

"What a mess, Fil."

Filomena stared down into the depths of her espresso. "I know."

"But you can't go on like this indefinitely. Sooner or later something or someone's going to have to give."

"I know," Filomena said again.

"How long can you go on fighting to make him take you on trust?"

"I don't know."

WHEN THE PHONE RANG in Trent's apartment Thursday evening, he leaped for it. For some idiotic reason he was sure it had to be Filomena. It wasn't. It was Gloria Paxton, and the woman was raging through her tears.

"He's gone to her," Gloria cried hysterically. "He left this afternoon. I didn't believe it at first, but now I do. That little tramp. She's finally won. After all these years, she's finally won. She was such a mousy little thing when she was a kid. A total zero in high school. A dumpy girl with no looks, no style, no boyfriends. She used to look so out of it most of the time. Never had a date. Oh, hell, how could she turn into such a...such a home-wrecker?" She broke off to sob brokenly.

Trent's hand became a vise on the phone. "Calm down, Gloria, and tell me exactly what's going on."

"I told you, Brady's left me. He's gone to her. She's lured him to Seattle so she can have her revenge on us. She doesn't even want him. She just wants to prove she can take him away from me the way I once took him away from her."

"What makes you think your husband has gone to Seattle?" Trent demanded sharply.

"He left a note," Gloria said in a strangled voice. "He said he'd made a mistake all those years ago when he married me instead of her. Said he felt stifled here in Gallant Lake. Said he wanted to change his life. The note said he was going to her because they still loved each other and . . . and . . . oh!" Gloria's voice trailed off into another spasm of hysterical weeping.

"Gloria, get hold of yourself," Trent advised in a voice that had been known to make seasoned corporate executives back off. Gloria was unfazed by the command.

"She'll do it, you know," she told Trent in broken tones. "You saw the way she was running around Gallant Lake half naked most of the time, driving that snazzy little car and showing off to the whole town. She wants revenge. She'll seduce him just to show us all that she can and then she'll toss him out on his ear. She doesn't really want him. She can do a lot better than him, and she knows it. But she's never forgiven me or Brady for what happened all those years ago, and she's finally going to get even."

Trent glanced impatiently at his watch. "When did your husband leave?"

"I don't know. I'm not sure. Sometime this afternoon. I got home from shopping and I found this stupid note." There was a ripping sound on the other end of the line as Gloria apparently tore the note into shreds. "I called you because I thought you ought to know what that little hussy is up to. She doesn't care who she hurts, does she? Or maybe she thinks she can seduce Brady and have her revenge and you'll never find out about it. At least I spiked her guns in that direction, didn't I?"

"My fiancée is not going to seduce your husband," Trent said in a savagely controlled voice. "You can stop worrying about that at any rate."

His absolute certainty on the subject seemed to get through to Gloria. "How can you be so blasted sure of that? She wants revenge, I tell you."

"I am sure of it because I'm sure of Filomena," Trent said coldly. "She's my fiancée, the woman I'm going to marry."

"So what? Brady was engaged to her when he fell in love with me and started sleeping with me! Being engaged doesn't mean anything. Neither does being married, for that matter."

Trent was getting more impatient by the minute. "You don't understand, Gloria, and I haven't got time to explain it. Just take my word for it. Your husband won't be spending tonight or any other night with Filomena."

Gloria was suddenly silent on the other end of the line. Trent's absolute conviction had made an impact. "Are . . . are you sure of that?"

"Positive. You have my word on the subject. Good-bye, Gloria." He hung up the phone before she could respond. Then he picked up the receiver again and dialed Filomena's number.

When there was no answer, he dialed the airport and got lucky. There was a jet leaving for Seattle in forty minutes.

FILOMENA WAS YAWNING as she got out of the elevator and walked down the hall to her apartment. The regular monthly dinner with Glenna and a few other women business friends had been fun, but the time had flown and she was pleasantly tired.

She wondered if Trent had tried to call during the evening. She'd forgotten to tell him she was going to be out. Serve him right if he'd called and gotten no answer. She didn't want him thinking she was sitting alone every evening pining for him.

She braced herself with that thought and fished the front door key out of her small sling bag. As she did so, a large male form detached itself from a doorway and came forward.

"'Bout time you got home. You must have one hell of a social life these days, huh, Fil? Not like the old days. Does Ravinder know where you go and who you see in the evenings?"

"Brady! What in the world are you doing here?" Filomena was so startled that she dropped the key on the carpet. Before she could grab it, Brady had it in his hand. He shoved it into the front door lock, his movements slightly uncoordinated and jerky. He had been drinking, she realized.

"I left Gloria," he announced grandly as he pushed open her front door and walked inside.

"What do you think you're doing? I didn't invite you in here, Brady. This is my apartment, and I want you out. Now." She scurried after him, leaving the door open behind her.

Brady threw himself into a chair and regarded her through narrowed eyes. There was a dangerous glitter in that gaze. Filomena was chillingly aware of just how much larger he was than she. It was strange, she thought. She'd never thought of Brady as potentially dangerous. But tonight she was no longer so sure. Any man who towered over her as Brady did was a potential hazard.

"Have a good time tonight, Fil? You sure run around a lot these days, don't you?"

"Have you been drinking?" she asked quietly.

"Had a few at a lounge down the street while I waited for you to get home," he said with a careless shrug.

"Brady..."

"Been a long time, Fil. I made the biggest mistake of my life when I married Gloria instead of you. I've finally realized that. But mistakes can be fixed. I'm going to fix this one. I'm ditching it all, Fil. Gloria, the kids, the business. Everything. Going to start over. Going to find myself. With you."

"Not a chance," Filomena said coolly. "I've already told you I'm not interested, Brady."

"Because you wangled an engagement with that honcho from Asgard Development? Forget him, Fil. That was just a business deal, and I know it. Heard all about that land you were going to get from your aunt and uncle when you married. But deep down inside you know it's me you love. You've never gotten over me. If we get married, you can still get the land. Knowing your uncle, it'll be a choice piece of property. I'm anxious to see it."

"You've definitely had a few too many," Filomena said, reaching for the phone. "I'm going to call you a cab."

"No," Brady said decisively, "I'm not leaving. I came here to be with you, Fil. I'm going to find out how much you've learned about men during the past few years."

11

"I WANT A SAMPLE of what you're giving Ravinder these days, Fil," Brady continued in slurred tones. "And I want a chance to show you what you've been missing with me."

"I haven't missed one single thing with you, Brady, and we both know it," Filomena said quietly. Her hand was on the phone.

"You want me. I know you do. *You still want me.* I left Gloria for you. You have to want me." He pounded his fist on the arm of the chair in which he was sitting, and something crumpled in his expression. The bold, aggressive male threat was gone. It was replaced by a frustrated, self-pitying anger.

"Gloria wants you, Brady. She wanted you when she was nineteen, and she wants you now. If you had any sense, you'd go back to her."

"I don't want her." The words were a childish plea.

"You wanted her at one time, Brady. You wanted her very much. Enough to sleep with her when you were engaged to me."

"She seduced me!"

Filomena shook her head. "Don't give me that. You were older than she was. You'd been through college. She was just a year out of high school, the same as me. You have to take the responsibility for any seducing that went on between the two of you. But you were never very good at taking responsibility, were you, Brady? You always wanted to take the easy path. Well, you took it and now you're stuck with it."

"It was you I loved, Fil. All along it was you I wanted."

"Love," she retorted scathingly. "You don't know the meaning of the word. You'd be better off not using it, especially around me. I know you too well, Brady."

"I've left her, Fil, don't you understand? I've left Gloria."

"That's your problem, not mine." Filomena began dialing a number she kept posted near the phone. She made her voice as forceful as possible, hoping it would penetrate his alcoholic haze. "I'm going to call you a cab. When it gets here, you're going to get into it and get out of my sight."

"No!"

"Then I will call the police."

He came up out of the chair just as she finished dialing the cab company's number. Instinctively Filomena jumped back, but her chair was in the way. Her ankle caught, and she fell to her knees just as Brady tried to take her into his arms. An instant later Brady collapsed on top of her. His weight crushed her painfully into the carpet.

Not for the first time in her life, Filomena cursed the fact that a large percentage of the population, especially the male population, was bigger than she was. She shoved with all her strength, but Brady was a deadweight on top of her.

"Get off of me," she snapped, punching him in the ribs.

"Ouch! Fil, please, just let me show you how good it could be between us now. I've got to kiss you—"

"Try it and I'll call the cops instead of a cab." Filomena stopped attempting to push him off and started trying to wriggle out from under him. It wasn't all that hard. Brady was big and heavy, but he wasn't particularly agile. Filomena used her fists again, and when he groaned and shifted his weight, she succeeded in rolling free of him.

"Damn it, Fil." Brady flopped over on his back, his arm covering his eyes in weary despair. "Why won't you give me a chance?"

Panting from exertion, Filomena ignored him and struggled to her knees. She straightened her clothes as she grabbed for the telephone. A steady hum on the line told her that the cab company dispatcher had hung up. She was about to dial again when she realized she and Brady were no longer alone in the room.

Startled, she glanced toward the door. Trent stood there, one hand braced against the jamb as he calmly took in everything from her disheveled clothing to Brady's prone figure on the carpet. Filomena froze. It couldn't get much worse than this, she thought, feeling entirely helpless. She just knelt there, staring at him and wondering why she had been such a fool to do battle with him over that piece of real estate. Perhaps if she'd given in on that, he wouldn't jump to conclusions now.

But she hadn't given in, and he was bound to think the worst now.

"Hello, Trent," she said with an aggressiveness she was far from feeling. "I'll bet you're wondering what's happening here, aren't you?"

"That's my Filomena," he responded mildly as he came through the door and strolled toward Brady. "Sassy and smart-mouthed right to the last. I'll give you credit for having the guts to defend an indefensible position. But, then, you never were short of guts." He halted beside Brady, gazing down at him as if he were examining a bug. "For everyone's information, I am not wondering what's happening here. I know exactly what's going on. I had a call from Gloria. She was kind enough to fill me in."

"That bitch." Brady took his arm away from his eyes and sat up cautiously. He glowered at Trent. "She had no right to call you."

"Paxton," Trent said as he reached down and yanked Brady to his feet by the lapels of his jacket, "you are turning into a damn nuisance."

Brady panicked and took what he saw as the logical way out. He nodded toward Filomena. "It was her fault. Blame your fancy fiancée. She lured me here. She wanted to seduce me."

Filomena stayed very still, holding her breath.

Trent slowly released his grip on Brady's lapels. "Is that right?" he asked, sounding amused. "Now why would she want to do that?"

Brady stepped back, jerking his shirt into place. He glared at Trent. "Why do you think? She wants me back. She used to be in love with me, and now she wants me back."

Trent gave him a slow, dangerous grin. "Paxton, you ass, if you believe that, you are a lot less intelligent than I originally thought, and believe me, I hadn't given you much credit to begin with."

"It's true!"

Trent shook his head. "I know the woman can be hard on a man's ego, but in this case I'm afraid you've got it coming. She doesn't want anything to do with you, Paxton."

It was too much for Brady. "How can you be so damn sure of that?" he roared, totally frustrated.

"Because she's engaged to me," Trent said quietly. "And Filomena would never fool around with another man behind her fiancé's back, not even for the sake of a little revenge." Trent turned his head and glanced at Filomena. "Who are you trying to call?"

"A cab," she managed to say. "For Brady."

"Well? What are you waiting for? Dial."

Filomena raised her brows at the command, but she decided this was not the time to argue about his tendency to give orders. She redialed the taxi company's number.

"Come with me, Paxton," Trent said as Filomena spoke to the dispatcher. "I'll make sure you get downstairs without having any unplanned falls down an elevator shaft."

Brady eyed Trent with open alarm. "Now wait just a minute," he began forcefully.

"It's all right, Brady," Filomena said, glancing up from the phone. "Trent will make sure you don't have any *planned* falls down elevator shafts, either, won't you, Trent?"

"You can trust me," Trent said, still smiling lethally. He gave Brady a slight shove toward the door. There didn't seem to be much weight behind the push, but the momentum carried Brady over the threshold and out into the hall. He ended up against the far wall and grabbed wildly for the duffel bag Trent tossed at him.

A moment later the door closed behind both men. Filomena hung up the phone and sat staring at her empty living room. Something was stunningly odd about the whole situation.

Trent should have been chewing nails and breathing fire. His rage should have been sufficient to shake the entire building. Instead, he seemed only mildly irritated by the whole, embarrassing scene. Furthermore, he had made it clear to Brady he knew Filomena would never cheat on him with another man.

The more she thought about it, the more she was forced to one simple conclusion. Trent might have a hangup about that stupid chunk of land, but he believed in her when it came to the important things.

Filomena heaved a deep sigh of relief and got to her feet.

When Trent opened the door a few minutes later and sauntered into the room, Filomena was waiting for him with a large, foaming mug of beer.

He dropped his jacket onto the nearest chair and took the mug from her hand. "Any other admirers hiding in the closets or under the bed?"

"No, Trent."

"Good. I think I've had about enough of Paxton, by the way. If I find him hanging around again I really might toss him down an elevator shaft."

"I'm sorry you found him here this time," Filomena said bluntly. "I didn't invite him."

He gave her a steady look. "I figured that out for myself."

"I'm . . . I'm glad," she said, feeling suddenly lighthearted and breathless. Her eyes were damp. "Thank you for trusting me, Trent. Not every man would have been as understanding in this sort of situation. I know how awful it must have looked."

"Do you?"

"Well, yes, I can imagine, and I realize what you must have thought when you got that call from Gloria. When I saw you standing there in the doorway, I was terrified you'd think the worst."

"I'll admit I am getting a little tired of pulling Brady Paxton off you."

Filomena winced. "But you honestly don't believe I invited him here?"

"I know you didn't."

His certainty was disturbing. "How can you be so sure?"

"Because you wouldn't do that to me," he said simply. "You're a little wild, too independent, inclined to be reckless and you can be a severe pain in the neck at times, but you fight fair, elf."

"Thanks. I think."

"You're welcome."

"Uh, Trent, if you didn't think I had lured Brady up here for revenge, why did you come dashing to the rescue?"

"I didn't think you'd invited Paxton, but I also didn't doubt for a minute that Gloria was right when she decided he was probably headed your way. I know it sounds old-fashioned and chauvinistic, but it occurred to me you might need rescuing. You're very small and very delicate, elf. Paxton outweighs you by about seventy or eighty pounds, and he's been stewing for weeks, wondering what he missed when he threw you back into the pond."

"You were worried about me?"

"I was irritated as hell with you. If you hadn't been so stubborn during the past few weeks, the situation would never have arisen in the first place. You would have been safely married to me by now."

Filomena smiled. "You really do want to marry me? After all the trouble I've caused you?"

"I don't know any other way to get some peace of mind." He raised the mug to his mouth. "How about that?" he said with pleased satisfaction after the first long swallow. "It's the real thing, not a light brew."

"I aim to please," she murmured, remembering how he had once said the same thing to her.

"The question is, how good is your aim?"

Filomena smiled tremulously. "I don't know. You tell me. And for the record, you can forget about the battle over the land my aunt and uncle want to give me. I never cared about it, anyway. It was just a principle I thought I had to defend, but I don't think I do any longer. I quit, you win. I surrender."

He regarded her for a long, thoughtful moment. "Too late. I gave up first."

Her eyes widened. "You *what*?"

"You heard me. Keep the land or sell it or grow Christmas trees on it. I don't care what you do with it."

"You don't?" she asked in disbelief.

"Nope."

"But, Trent, you can't do this to me. This is my big scene," she protested, caught between laughter and tears of relief. *He didn't care about the land.*

"I know," he said dryly. "And you're so good at causing scenes, aren't you? But this time you've been upstaged." He took another long swallow of beer and set the mug down on a nearby table. "About time somebody did it."

She hesitated another split second and then she hurled herself into his arms. "Trent, do you mean that? You really don't care about the land?"

He wrapped his arms around her and buried his face in her hair. "I knew when Gloria phoned me with her big news about Brady heading north to Seattle that I didn't care about the land. It was just the principle of the thing for me, too. Deep down I didn't care about anything except getting you tied to me legally, emotionally and permanently. I trust you, Filomena, my sweet elf. You're probably going to drive me crazy during the next sixty years, but I trust you."

"Oh, Trent, I love you so much. I was so afraid of what you'd think when you walked in here a few minutes ago and found Brady. I could have killed him for turning up here the way he did."

"The thought crossed my mind a couple of times on the way down to the lobby," Trent admitted.

"The thought of me killing Brady?"

"No, the thought of me killing him. But ultimately I decided he just wasn't worth it."

"That's exactly the conclusion I came to shortly after I found him and Gloria in bed together," Filomena admitted.

"Isn't it great to start marriage off with someone with whom you have so much in common?" Trent lifted her chin and kissed her with a thoroughness that left no room for doubt.

TWO WEEKS LATER Trent settled himself against the pillows of the wide hotel bed and glanced impatiently at the watch he had unstrapped earlier and left on the bedside table. Ten more minutes had gone by since the last time he had checked the time. Filomena still hadn't come out of the bathroom. She'd been in there over forty-five minutes.

Trent closed his eyes and willed himself to be patient. This was Filomena's wedding night. She had a right to some privacy and all the time she needed to get ready. Just because he was already experiencing a dull, sweet ache in his loins didn't mean he had the right to forge his way into the bathroom and drag his bride into bed. She would arrive in her own time.

Elf time.

Trent's fingers drummed a small tattoo on the bed beside him. He opened his eyes and took another look at the face of his watch. This was getting ridiculous. He made another bid for patience, occupying himself with memories of Filomena walking serenely down the aisle toward him a few hours earlier. It was a charming memory, one he would treasure for the rest of his life.

The small wedding had taken place that morning. Filomena's beaming family and the equally pleased staff of the lodge had been in attendance. Trent grinned briefly, recalling the relief he had detected behind the warm, loving smiles on everyone's face. Getting Filomena safely married had taken a burden of worry off a great many shoulders. Amery and Meg Cromwell as well as Aunt

Agnes and Uncle George, Shari and Jim had all come up to Trent privately during the small reception, not only to wish him good luck, but to commend him on his bravery.

"Just remember, this sale is final," Amery had said cheerfully. "No refunds and no returns."

Trent knew that more than one person in the small chapel had held his or her breath waiting to see what Filomena would wear to her own wedding. She had kept it a secret from everyone except Shari. Meg Cromwell's sigh of relief had almost been audible when her eldest daughter had come down the aisle dressed in a demure, ballet style, calf-length dress that had emphasized her slenderness and made her look like a fairy queen dressed for a secret moonlight dance. Her red hair had cascaded down her back beneath a wispy veil that had been draped from a stylish garden party hat. Trent had seen the loving laughter in her eyes as she had peeked out at him from under the brim of the hat and had thanked his lucky stars she hadn't chosen to wear scarlet red or slinky black. Elves were unpredictable.

The sound of running water in the bathroom jerked Trent out of his reminiscences. He checked his watch again. The water was shut off, but the bathroom door didn't open. Silence descended once more.

Trent waited another few minutes and then reached the end of his patience. Wedding night privacy for the bride was one thing; the extended and unexplained absence of his elf from her bridal bed required a few answers, however. He strode across the room, naked except for his briefs, and rapped on the bathroom door.

"Filomena? Honey, what's going on in there?"

"Nothing."

Trent's eyes narrowed. "Are you sure?"

"Of course I'm sure."

"Are you okay?"

"I'm fine."

Trent paused. "Are you intending to spend your entire wedding night in the bathroom?"

"No."

Another pause. When there was no further explanation, Trent asked bluntly, "What's taking so long?"

"I'm getting dressed."

"Filomena, this is your wedding night. You're supposed to be getting undressed," Trent finally said in exasperation.

"Brides get to wear peignoirs. I might never again have an excuse to wear one, so I want to get the most out of this experience."

He heard the lilting amusement in her voice and decided enough was enough. If she was going to tease him, she could do it in bed. Trent put his hand on the doorknob and twisted. She hadn't locked it.

The door popped open easily enough and revealed Filomena standing in the center of the bathroom in front of a full-length mirror. Her face was hidden beneath a cloud of soft apricot-colored silk that she was in the process of removing. On the floor around her feet were several other crumpled piles of gossamer, silky fabric. Discarded nightgowns, ranging in color from iridescent emerald green to shimmering silver, littered the bathroom like so much expensive wrapping paper.

"Trent!" At the sound of the bathroom door being opened, Filomena struggled frantically to get the apricot confection back down over her head. "What are you doing in here? I'm getting ready for bed."

Trent folded his arms and leaned against the wall. He watched the dusky rose of two pert nipples disappear beneath the apricot gown. Then the delicate fabric slipped down over her hips, hiding the most intimate part of her.

"You're not getting ready for bed," Trent decided. "You're putting on a fashion show."

Filomena smiled benignly. "I couldn't decide which one to bring with me, so I packed a whole bunch. I've been trying them all on to see which one looks best."

Trent came away from the door, reaching for his bride before she could sidestep him.

"You surprise me, elf," he said gently. "Somehow I hadn't expected to see you succumb to an attack of wedding night nerves."

"I am not nervous," she declared haughtily as his hands settled on her shoulders. She looked up at him, unaware of the hint of anxiety that was in her eyes.

Trent smiled. "Are you sure?"

"I'm sure."

"What if I told you that I'm a little nervous?"

Her eyes widened. "Are you?" She reached up to touch the side of his face, her fingers light and comforting on his skin.

"No, but I thought it might make you feel better if you thought you weren't the only one with butterflies." He laughed down at her and swooped.

"Trent, put me down," Filomena squeaked, her voice filled with laughter as he lifted her off her feet and tucked her under his arm. "I've got three other gowns to try on."

"If you think I'm going to spend my wedding night watching a fashion show, you've got a lot to learn about me, honey." He stood her on her feet beside the bed and grasped the apricot gown. With one long, firm movement he jerked it off over her head and dropped it on the rug. "That's better." His hands went to her bare waist and he pulled her against his chest. "Much better."

Filomena sighed and wrapped her arms around his neck. "I suppose I can try the gowns on some other time."

"Uh-huh." He ignored that, his mind on the clamoring desire skyrocketing through him. He felt her small breasts pillowed against him and knew an immediate, flaring response. "I can't believe I've finally got you, elf. Where have you been all my life?"

"Waiting for you," she said simply. She put her mouth against his chest, planting tiny, warm kisses on his hot skin.

Trent groaned and pushed his leg between her thighs, opening her to his touch. He could feel the rising heat in her and an exciting, feminine dampness that made the blood pound in his veins.

Filomena whispered his name, her lips moving on his skin as she clung to him. She opened her eyes and looked up at him with love and longing and an infinite promise as he lifted her and settled her onto the turned-back bed.

For a long moment their gazes locked in silent understanding and commitment.

"I love you," Trent finally said, his voice husky with need.

"I love you." She touched his shoulder with delicate nails and stirred beneath his weight. Her leg moved to twine around his muscled thigh.

"I know, my love. I know." Trent lowered his head and took her lips, secure at last in the magic that had invaded his world.

JULIE ELLIS

author of the bestselling
Rich Is Best rivals the likes of
Judith Krantz and Belva Plain with

THE ONLY SIN

It sweeps through the glamorous cities of Paris, London, New York and Hollywood. It captures life at the turn of the century and moves to the present day. *The Only Sin* is the triumphant story of Lilli Landau's rise to power, wealth and international fame in the sensational fast-paced world of cosmetics.

IF GEORGIA BOCKOVEN CAPTURED YOU ONCE, SHE'LL DO IT AGAIN!

In Superromance #246, *Love Songs*, Amy had to protect her friend, Jo, from all the Brad Tylers of the world. Now in Temptation #161, *Tomorrow's Love Song*, Amy has her own troubles brewing....

She assumes a false identity and sets out to right a few wrongs. She's got everything to gain—millions of dollars. And everything to lose—the one man who belongs in her future....

Look for Temptation #161, *Tomorrow's Love Song*. Coming to you in July!

Harlequin Temptation

COMING NEXT MONTH

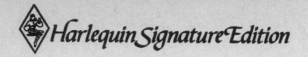

Carole Mortimer

Merlyn's Magic

She came to him from out of the storm and was drawn into his yearning arms—the tempestuous night held a magic all its own.

You've enjoyed Carole Mortimer's Harlequin Presents stories, and her previous bestseller, *Gypsy*.

Now, don't miss her latest, most exciting bestseller, *Merlyn's Magic*!

IN JULY

MERMG